MAMLUK

Emergence

By James Jackson

Printed by Amazon

Cover Design by Jason Williams

ISBN: 978-1-941-590-22-5

Author's Works

Terran Chronicles Universe

Novels

First Contact
Discovery
Colony
Alliance
Voknor Diaries

Short Stories

Johnny's Jaunt
Pythos
Jie's World
End of Times
Sharz Affect
Joes Notes: Gamin Technology Journal
Emma's Legacy

Lands of Phrey

The Dark Warlock Trilogy

Other Works

Mamluk
America – Democracy at a Crossroads
Augmented Reality

Dedication

Acknowledgements

Many thanks to my wife, Jairis, for listening to my ramblings as I continue to tap away at my keyboard and turn thoughts and ideas into words.

A special thank you goes to Shannon and Jeff, who continue to tirelessly review and edit my works. I greatly appreciate the vast amount of time, energy, and effort, they have contributed over the years.

Gratitude to Michael for his input into the creature, Mamluk, and to Brandon whose feedback has been invaluable.

Another person I must thank is my longtime friend, Jason. His dedication, website design work and video creation, is greatly appreciated.

Table of Contents

Preface

We live in a constant state of preparedness, whether it be for war, or natural disaster. Consequently, we spend a vast amount of resources on weapons we don't expect to use, and stockpile food and medical supplies for calamities that we hope will never take place. What if a race were to exist in this state for thousands of years? What would the people of this culture be like? Would they strive to better themselves, and the society they live in, or would atrophy set in?

"Captivity is the greatest of evils that can befall one." - Miguel de Cervantes

"The chance is now given you to end in a day the bondage of centuries, and to ride in one bound from social degradation to the place of common equality with all other varieties on men." - Frederick Douglas

I hereby welcome you all to, 'Mamluk'.

This is a work of fiction, or is this our ultimate destiny?
I hope you, the reader, enjoy this as much as I have enjoyed writing it.
James Jackson

Introduction Part I

The first Emperor of the Atlan Protectorate, Leroy Jenson, faced many difficult choices. His battered and beleaguered crew found themselves on the threshold of extinction as destiny forced them to play the role laid out thousands of years before.

The first planet of the Protectorate was a pristine world; one filled with an abundance of animal and plant life. A single indigenous species showed promise of one day rising up to be the intellectual masters of their world, but the arrival of Leroy's forces forever changed their destiny. Dubbed 'silent death' by Leroy's crew, these powerful predators were the apex of the planet's food chain.

At two meters in length, these digitigrades moved as well on all fours, as they did upright on their powerful hindquarters. Their near-black skin consisted of interlocking scales with miniscule hairs on them. These dragon-like scales flexed with their movements, and hardened when exposed to extreme temperatures, or threats. These scales were as light and tough as titanium, yet remained flexible. The males of the species fought savagely to be the leaders of the packs which roamed freely across the planet's vast tracts of land. Their rear paws had five long claws, four front and one rearward. The rear claw was used as a weapon, providing grip when on soft soil, or for climbing steep embankments. Some creatures were even reported as being able to climb trees. Their front paws also had five razor sharp claws, which they would use to flail open the stomachs of their prey within seconds of bringing them down. Immense herds of various four-legged beasts roamed the lush planet, providing an abundance of food for these ferocious predators.

These sturdy animals were not as heavy as they appeared to be. Their bones were as strong, and light, as carbon steel, while their muscles were filled with carbon-like filaments. Damaged scales flaked off their bodies, revealing a replacement below which would quickly fill with nutrients, and be as robust as the original within a day or two.

Their heads were bobcat-like, with long ears that could either lay flat against their skulls, or extend up and swivel, pinpointing their prey with great precision. Their short snouts were filled with razor sharp teeth, and topped with a small, keen, nose. Their eyes were another amazing feature. Their round, grey irises, were large, with a crosshair at the center. A small area of white surrounded the irises, while two independent eyelids protected their eyes. When diving into water, the thin secondary lids would close, restricting their ability to see, but not completely eliminating it. These animals had amazing vision and could see in the infrared and ultra-violet spectrums, in addition to normal sight. Their brains processed all signals simultaneously, providing them with an acute image of their prey.

Emperor Jenson was faced with a dilemma. His crew was all that stood between them and extinction, and they were too few to both establish their presence, and to begin subjugating other worlds. Hearing tales of the ferocious predator on the planet they chose to call home, gave him an idea. His scientists captured a live creature, and began modifying its genetic code, ultimately creating the perfect killing machine. These genetically modified creatures were sterile. Once they had completed their task of eradicating the indigenous populations of worlds they were deposited upon, they died out. This left the planet open to a safe conquest by advanced cleanup parties who prepared the planet for the second wave, the colonists. This system was so effective, it remained in place, with few changes, for millennia. With few internal issues, no major diseases, and an expendable military, the Protectorate's population exploded.

These ground forces of the Atlan Protectorate were named, 'Mamluk', and they still exist to this day.

Introduction Part II

It is the year 7578 of the Atlan Protectorate, and the time of Emperor Tyron. The Protectorate is an isolationist empire, one that encompasses thousands of worlds within the galactic core. Its borders are so heavily guarded that no spacecraft has ever breached its defenses, nor returned from whence they came. The vast majority of the Protectorate's trillions of people go about their daily routines, blissfully unaware of the politics involved in maintaining their extensive Empire.

The Protectorate's leadership maintains a distant watch over the Atlan Empire. Apart for the issuance of the twelve prophesies long ago, of which one is revealed every thousand years, the Protectorate takes great effort not to interfere with any of its galactic neighbors. The Protectorate's goal of a slow expansion and non-interference seem at odds with each other. Yet it has worked all this time to keep the Empire safe from invasion and preserve the precious timeline.

The defense grid that surrounds the Empire consists of an incalculable number of automatic systems, backed by mammoth space stations, and equally large construction facilities. This border is not static but is constantly moving outward. The speed of this expansion is imperceptible to the naked eye, yet numerous space-factories churn out a steady stream of defense platforms to fill gaps in the grid as it expands. Approaching spacecraft are met with an instant, and overwhelming, volley of firepower. Any vessel attempting to leave the Protectorate is deemed hostile and dealt with accordingly.

Communication with 'outsiders' is strictly forbidden, and although this is a topic of debate at times, the leadership remains resolute in their stance. The idea that a plan would last thousands of years is difficult for most to grasp.

There are few prisons within the Empire, as virtually all crimes are punishable by death. Every citizen is required to perform four years of public service for the Empire. Many perform this duty on far flung space stations, or communications arrays.

Prologue

Station LJX-417.876

Mildgyd yawns, then stretches in his chair as he rubs his tired eyes. Although he has only been at this remote space monitoring facility for two weeks, staring at a blank display has already become a tedious duty. He turns to his two colleagues, and asks flatly, "Are you two bored yet?" He lifts his eyebrows as he runs his appraising gaze up and down the attractive woman who stands in the room.

Athena is tall and is as intelligent as she is stunning. Her hazel eyes sparkle energetically beneath her long blond hair. Her fair skin appears flawless, while her perfectly formed white teeth seem to glow. She chuckles at his intense gaze, nudges Peyton, the well-built man standing next to her, and says, "Why, I think our new boy here likes me!"

Peyton joins in her laughter, points to Mildgyd and says, "Good luck rookie, she cycles out next run."

Mildgyd gazes around the small room, sighs, then says, "So, what am I supposed to do here?"

Peyton grins, waves his arms around the control room, and then says, "Welcome to tracking station LJX-417876."

Mildgyd stops gawking and returns his gaze to the display before him. He frowns, tilts his head in curiosity, then says, "Does anything ever come up on this thing?"

Athena slowly shakes her head from side to side and replies, "I have been on this outpost for almost four years, and I have never seen a thing."

Mildgyd points to the display and asks inquisitively, "So... what's that then?"

Peyton steps forward, gazes at the display, and says arrogantly, "Okay rookie, what did you do?" He stares at the display, and particularly at a red dot that is moving across it. With a frown forming on his brow he turns and glances at Athena, then says, "System check on main display."

The outpost's computer system quickly and efficiently responds, "Confirmed. The main display is functioning as specified."

"Uh," Peyton stammers, then asks, "Well then, what is that dot?"

"Unknown vessel on escape trajectory," replies the station's computer.

Athena's jaw drops, "Escape trajectory?" She repeats, turning to Peyton with her mouth open, a chill running up her spine.

Mildgyd blinks in surprise. He is not sure if they are pulling some joke, but as he looks at them, he becomes more alarmed. The hair rises on the back of his neck when he realizes that this is not some prank. He asks apprehensively, "So what's our procedure?"

Athena and Peyton stare at each other in bewilderment, but neither of them moves.

"Confirmed," intones the computer system, "receiving instructions."

Mildgyd reads the words before him slowly and deliberately, "Level eleven event, containment protocol engaged." He glances at the others and asks, "What's a level eleven event?"

Athena shrugs her shoulders, then says, "I have no idea."

"Confirmed." Intones the computer system once again. "Level eleven event; failure of a class one transport to maintain flight plan during transfer of biologics."

Peyton stares at Athena and says, "Damn, I knew these computers were equipped with adaptive receptors, but I'm impressed."

The three of them watch as the red blip passes them; its flight path clearly taking the small vessel toward the periphery of the Empire.

Peyton says uneasily, "If they don't turn around, we'll get to see how the defense grid works."

Athena nods in agreement, then asks curiously, "System, when you say biologics, what do you mean?"

"Confirmed." Responds the computer, "The transport manifest indicates a single, generation five, Mamluk."

The three of them are baffled by the response, and simply stare at each other. Mildgyd breaks the silence and asks, "What the blazes is a Mamluk?" He glances around then asks, "System, what is a Mamluk?"

"Confirmed." intones the station's computer, "Mamluk: Biologically engineered species."

Athena taps her fingers in annoyance at the seemingly obstinate computer, then says, "System, what is their function?"

When the expected reply does not greet their ears Peyton speaks up, "System, what can you tell us about these Mamluk?"

The computer responds immediately, "Confirmed; further information pertaining to subject matter is classified."

The crew of the tracking station stares at the defense grid as it powers up and targets the escaping vessel. Mildgyd stares and wonders what a Mamluk is, and what a transport shuttle is doing this far away from the core worlds.

Chapter One – Awareness

The rush of information would overwhelm most, but not me, for I am Mamluk. Information on navigation, piloting, life support, and more, floods into my mind, and in doing so creates a semi-euphoric feeling. The stasis pod cycles through its pre-programmed emergency routine, and then opens with a hiss of escaping gas.

I slowly flex my muscular arms and legs before stepping out from my near vertical pod. I glance around and see three other pods which, upon closer inspection, prove to be empty. Striding to the closed cockpit door I begin to take huge breaths in the hopes that hyperventilating will not make this a short walk. According to what I have just learned, the area beyond is open to space, and airless.

I stop, then purge most of the atmosphere in my area before opening the door. The rush of air as the door opens is not excessive but ruffles my short black hair as it passes. I quickly scan the cockpit, knowing I have mere minutes to find the hull breach, and seal it, before I die.

Both pilots are slumped forward in their seats, held in place by their safety harnesses. Numerous flashing lights indicate several system failures, but none of these are as important as finding the leak. Looking straight ahead reveals stars, real stars. A section of the forward view is completely missing, revealing open space. I can already feel the coldness having an impact as the moisture in my eyes begins to freeze. I force my secondary lids to close, and even though this restricts my vision, it will afford me more time. My body's interlocked scales harden in an attempt to protect my core from exposure.

I already know where the emergency repair kit is and reach for it without looking. Opening the kit reveals a mirror, and a limited supply of what some desk-jockey would call, essentials.

If I make it through this, I will be paying someone a visit, I think vehemently.

Three small rubber-like patches and one can of sealant, along with a few tools are all there is in the kit. It takes all three patches, the entire can of spray, and the body of one of the pilots to suitably block the hole. As I finish my task, I can feel the edges of darkness creeping upon my eyes. My lungs begin to scream out for air, while a numbness begins to work its way up my arms and legs.

Pressurizing the cockpit takes more time, during which I take shallow breaths of the thin air as it fills the space. The heaters have been running at one hundred percent in an effort to maintain the cockpit's temperature and are the only reason I did not freeze. Well, I guess I can live for ten minutes in a near vacuum.

I stare at the empty chair and shake my head. My knee joints bend in the opposite direction as the pilots', making sitting in the chairs problematic. I grip the empty chair, then with all my might, rock it back and forth, tearing it from the floor. Tossing the chair to one side, I stand before the console and review the data.

It only takes me a moment to discover that a tracking station has already classified my craft as a target to be eliminated. Luckily, they are only a listening post. The real weapons are still ahead, though sensors show that they are turning this way.

I quickly scan the nearest planet, and to my surprise, find that not only is it habitable, the Protectorate has yet to establish its presence there. Leaning on the console, I deftly turn the ship, and engage full power to the engines. The trip will take a few hours, giving me time to properly inspect my surroundings. Fortunately, the planet is inside the Protectorate's defense grid, and too insignificant to be worthy of any attention.

A careful examination of my hands reveals little sign of exposure to the elements. I flex each of my fingers, one at a time, then each of the claws of my feet. Next, I locate the craft's medical kit, and examine my eyes in its mirror. My crosshair shaped pupils expand and contact as they should. There is a tinge of redness to the grey outer color, indicating a few minor blood vessels have ruptured, but they should heal.

Checking the sensors, I notice that the distant weapons pods are still tracking my shuttle, but they do not fire.

Finding out what happened to the shuttle is easy. According to the ship's sensors, a rogue meteoroid penetrated the shields, and then blew a hole in the craft's central window. The Protectorate's reliance on shields instead of armor, is why the hull breach occurred. Noticing why the shields failed to protect the craft alarms me, the craft's main power cell is almost empty. The last recharge reported an error, which the pilots failed to notice, or perhaps they ignored. I shake my head as I wonder about their complacency. Who flies on a near empty power cell?

Approaching the planet, I perform a basic scan, and am pleased to find it teeming with life, some of which is intelligent. The discovery that the most advanced species is humanoid, but also utilizes domesticated animals as transport, brings both joy, and disappointment. While this means that I will not be detected, it also means that the inhabitants will not develop the industry required to recharge my power cell, or to repair the damaged window for quite some time. I shake my head as more information appears on my screen. The technology level of the indigenous populace is woeful. A few isolated areas of the planet have primitive looking towns with signs of early metallurgy. But most of the remaining inhabitants rove the continents in nomadic bands.

I review the planet's basic statistics impassionedly. Its gravity is slightly lower, and its day-night cycle shorter, than the Atlan Standard. The atmosphere is breathable, and well within survival tolerances. The world's oceans and waters are a mystery and will require a physical analysis prior to drinking.

I glance at the power indicator, and cringe. I will be able to land, but that is about it. Swinging the craft into a high orbit. I take a complete sensor scan of the planet, and then commence my descent.

Touchdown

The most stable region of the planet is also the largest continent. I fly toward its northern region, where ancient glacial movements and water flows have carved a swath down a mountain range. All that remains of the glacier is a small lake atop a distant mountain. A stream meanders from this lake, along the floor of the valley, and past the numerous cave entrances dotting the neighboring hills.

Scanning these caves confirms my findings, and my decision. I select the largest of them and fly inside. Turning the craft around, I back it up between two massive rock outcroppings, near a side wall, and then land. I shut down the crafts near depleted power unit, casting everything into dark shadows as the interior lights go out.

I exit the craft, walk outside the cave and sniff the air. The oxygen-hydrogen mix is slightly richer than I am used to. Various four-legged animals graze on the grasslands, while many species of avian fills the skies. None of these creatures pay me any heed. The nearest settlement is many days away on foot, though it is obvious that the indigenous population traverses this valley. The scent of old campfires lingers in many of the nearby caves.

I stare at the grazing beasts and wonder if they will provide the same sustenance as the food cubes. The idea of killing a beast to eat is not what bothers me, the issue is whether or not I should cook the meat.

I turn back to the cave, and then begin to put into place my long-term plan. I eat and drink a two-day supply of rations, and then remove the bodies of the pilots. One of them wears a utility belt, which I put on. Its half dozen pouches contain a variety of incidentals. I stare at the items in confusion, and then place them on the remaining seat. I will have to figure out what they are later.

I carry the bodies outside, and then look for a suitable place to bury them. Finding none, I use a piece of the discarded pilot's chair as a shovel and dig a deep hole in rear of my cave. I unceremoniously dump the corpses in the pit, and then refill the hole.

Next, I carefully move rocks and boulders, and place them in front of the transport. The shadows lengthen across the valley as I labor to complete my task. With the sun's last rays fading, I stop to examine my efforts. I am pleased to see that the craft is no longer visible, and as I had hoped, the two rocky outcroppings, now look like one massive, and natural, pile of boulders. Climbing to the top, I look down at the craft, and smile. I realize that I will have to cover the craft completely, but for now, it is out of sight from anyone wandering into the cave.

I climb down, stride outside, and stare into the darkness. The grazing animals are still visible as thermal images. I look upward, and then begin the long climb up the steep, rocky, hillside. It takes much of the night, but eventually I arrive at the top. The star filled sky looks so close, I feel as though I could almost touch it.

A new smell suddenly assaults my nose. I spin toward it, senses on full alert, and scowl. One of the many roving bands I detected from space, has established a campsite in a valley parallel to the one with my cave. I notice a dozen crude tents, and forty or so pack animals. Approximately thirty individuals gather around a large fire, roasting a large animal on a massive spit. I sit and watch them carefully. They look a lot like Atlans, only a little taller, more muscular, darker skinned, and with longer dark hair which some of them have braided. Whenever one of them approaches the massive fire, the thermal images blend. They are too distant for me to discern any more details. Finally, they retire to sleep. I am puzzled when I see three of them stay awake, as sentries. As the night crawls by, the sentries wake others, and then sleep themselves. I wonder what they are guarding against.

With the early morning sun peeking over the distant horizon, I make sure that I am well concealed as I watch the campsite. They take their time packing up their animal skin tents. Food must be easily obtained as they leave the remnants of their meal behind. By mid-morning the group is travelling. They follow the valley next to the one I chose and seem to be in no hurry to get anywhere. I cautiously follow the ridge as I monitor their progress. When they are well past where the back of my cave would be, I decide it is time to rest, and return to the shuttle.

I eat a great feast of food cubes, drink copious amounts of water from the shuttle's stores, then power up my pod, and sleep in it. Even though the craft's power cell indicator is hovering at its lowest point, my pod requires little energy. I set my sleep cycle for a single day, and then activate the pod's instruction program to teach me all I need to know about planetary survival. Due to the low power level, the pods casing remains open, and its environmental controls stay offline.

Base Camp

I wake up feeling refreshed, and grin. I now know how to make fire, build basic shelters, and craft rudimentary weapons. More importantly, the scans I took on the way down indicate that the local life will sustain me, whether I cook it or not.

I exit the shuttle, carefully climb the rock wall, and then cautiously step out of the cave. Knowing that roving bands inhabit, or at the very least, traverse these valleys, heightens my awareness. I glance at the rapidly moving clouds, and frown. A breeze begins, and soon strengthens into powerful gusts. A lightning bolt strikes the mountains on the far side of the valley. A loud booming sound quickly follows. Seconds later, large drops of water fall from the sky. The rain fall is brief, but violent. I retreat into my cave and discover why it has gone unused by the local inhabitants. Its large entrance allows the rain and wind to whip inside, drenching virtually the entire area. Observing this delights me; it is doubtful that this cave will see much traffic in the future.

Once the storm passes, I make my way to the cave nearest mine and examine it. When I find no signs of habitation or use, I check the next, and then the next. I eventually find what I am looking for, a cave with an old campfire. This will be the cave that I cook my meals in. Feeling smug at my thoughtfulness, I glance down at the cave's floor. A chill runs up and down my spine. All I can see are my footprints, with their deep claw marks. I follow my own prints from the cave and to my alarm clearly see them leading in and out of every cave that I have examined. It takes me the rest of the day to remove all signs of my passage.

I eat another batch of food cubes, and then retire to my pod once more. This time I instruct the computer to instruct me in stealth and tracking techniques. It would seem that I was not properly trained.

Waking, I feel relaxed and rejuvenated. I check the transport's power cell, and sigh. There is enough energy left to operate the pod for many weeks, but as for getting off the ground, that is problematic. I recall a segment of my training, open a panel in the pilot area, and remove a utility pack. Inside are; additional medical supplies, a small tool kit, and a solar powered distress beacon. Next to the pack rests a crate of food cubes. I take four of these, eat one, and place the rest in a pouch on my belt.

Once again, I cautiously exit the cave and scrutinize my surroundings. Animals graze the prairieland, while birds flit about overhead. I glance at the claws on my feet and grin. I take off at a lope, heading downwind of the grazing animals. A few minutes later I swing back, and sprint toward them with all my might. They scatter in panic, with one of them running almost straight at me. I catch its throat with the extended claws from my left hand as it attempts to whip by me. The beast's throat flails open, spurting blood in great gushes as its heart beats futilely. It collapses to the ground, dead. The others stare at their fallen comrade, then return to grazing as if nothing had happened.

I carry the carcass to the cave with the old campfire and get to work. I skin the beast, build a fire and then cook its meat. The meat has an unexpectedly pleasant flavor, unlike the food cubes which now seem bland by comparison.

I take the animal skin down to the creek, and thoroughly soak it. I then grind up the three food cubes and smear the crumbs onto the wet hide. According to the computer this will aid in curing the hide, which makes me wonder what is in them. I decide that I do not really want to know and carry on until the entire hide is covered in a thin layer of paste. I set the hide on a rock in the sun to dry, and then return to my cave.

I spend the rest of the afternoon carefully arranging huge rocks to block off a portion of the front of my cave. I pack the gaps with sand and soil. I climb to a point above the newly formed wall and create a small landslide, effectively adding a natural looking effect to the wall. With the sun's last rays, I retire into the shuttle once more.

The next morning as I exit the craft, a strange musky smell assaults my nose. I cautiously climb the rock wall, and then peer over the top. A massive four-legged beast is pacing around. The creature's tan fur ripples as its muscles move. It sniffs the air, then turns and looks straight at me. Its ears flatten on its head as it bares its teeth and growls. Its yellow eyes narrow, while the whiskers on its short snout raise. The cat-like creature backs away warily, growling loudly. The animal is almost as large as me, and judging by its massive paws, could probably put up a good fight.

I leap on top of the rock wall and roar at the beast as loudly as I can, exposing my own razor-sharp teeth. The creature flees, its paws skid and slide as its legs move too fast for the sandy surface. With one last growl, the creature bolts out the cave's entrance.

I step outside and see the large cat lingering in the distance, warily watching me. I watch as the beast cautiously approaches the cave with the remnants of my previous day's meal. The beast pads inside, then exits moments later with the entire carcass in its jaws. The animal drags its find to the creek and begins to eat.

Ignoring the beast for now, I examine my cave's entrance. I change my mind about closing it off, and even though my new idea will take some time to implement, I feel that it is the best option. Before I work on my plan for the cave, I kill another beast, cook and eat some, and then prepare its hide. I carry this carcass outside and leave it.

Each day sees the entrance to my cave becoming smaller and smaller as I meticulously work at it. I build two adjacent walls, so that anyone entering must traverse a sharp bend. The outer wall curves back toward the hillside and, from virtually any angle, does not appear to be a cave entrance at all anymore. Stepping inside the dark narrow confines, the cavity appears to end, and only by walking down it can the bend be seen. In addition, this second narrow walkway slopes upward toward the roof, so much so that I must crouch in order to get through. As a final touch, I build a fire-pit outside the wall, and away from the opening. Hopefully this perpetuates the impression that there is insufficient room inside.

Three weeks pass before I have all that I need, and the cave's entrance is now thoroughly concealed. During this time, I kill many grazing animals, and begin preserving the meat for future use. These dried out strips are tough and salty, but will provide a supplement to the remaining food cubes. I leave the carcasses for the cat-like creature to drag away. Some days the animal actually seems to be waiting for me to provide its food.

Surprisingly, the shuttle's computer continues to operate, and provides training as I sleep in my pod. As I learn more about the shuttle, I disable several its passive functions; life support, gravity, interior lights, and the pilot stations. Although these were switched off, they were still drawing a minute amount of power.

The first of the hides has been smoked and is finally ready for use. This hide will become my footwear. It takes me all day to make the sandals, but eventually I can slide my feet into them. Walking around in them takes some getting used to, and they leave some pretty decent footprints. I hope that if anyone sees these prints, they will assume they have simply been left by a large individual, which is preferable to the tracks I was leaving before.

I continue to learn from the training computer and put more of that knowledge to the test. I take the solar powered distress beacon and open it up. Next, I remove a bundle of wires from one of the other pods. I then go to the pilot area and open a panel that exposes the ship's power grid. It takes all day, but eventually I have run wires from the pilot area, and out through the front of the cave. I have to cannibalize two other pods in order to obtain enough wiring. I dig a small depression, and then place the beacon in it. Thanks to a rocky outcropping it is not visible from the either the ridgeline above, or the valley below. I connect one end of the wiring to the distress beacon's solar panel, after making sure the beacon itself is offline, and then cover the cable with dirt.

I follow and cover the cable all the way to the shuttle, where, via a makeshift fuse, I connect the other end to the power grid. A steady stream of power now flows into the shuttle's energy cell. My nightly use of the pod will still draw more energy than the solar panel can collect in a day, however, if I stop using the pod, the shuttle's power reserve will slowly fill.

In an effort to protect the shuttle, animal skins now cover its thruster ports, the missing central window, and main drive casing. Over time the dust and dirt would build up, and eventually ruin the systems I hope to use one day.

I have finally learned how to use the shuttle's analyzer and take water samples from the stream. The results exceed my wildest expectations. The water is filled with naturally occurring electrolytes and minerals. As soon as I get the results, I begin to transport water to the shuttle and refill its storage tank. The tank will filter the water of any harmful bacteria and keep it fresh. The setting sun is a stark reminder that this planet's cycle is slightly shorter than what I consider as normal. I decide to retire for the night anyway.

I step from my pod refreshed and stretch. I frown when a familiar muskiness assaults my nose. I cautiously make my way to the top of the makeshift wall between the shuttle and the main cave area. No light enters the cave anymore; however, my thermal vision easily detects the massive beast which has been taking the spent carcasses. It swings its head from me, to the narrow opening halfway up the inner wall I built, and then back. I turn my head and see five smaller images, its young, I presume.

I stare at the scene, perplexed. Why would this creature bring its young in here? Then I hear it, voices from the cave entrance.

I skirt my way around the beast, slowly making my way to the narrow entryway. I quietly make my way down the passageway, and turn the corner, coming face to face with a tribesman.

The man screams as he reaches for a weapon of sorts. I shove him to the ground, and then while pinning his chest with my hands, rake his stomach with my rear claws. Warm blood gushes from his body as his screams change pitch. I glance up in time to see another tribesman standing at the entrance. The light from outside creates an odd halo effect around the man.

I can sense the man's fear as he steps back. Without hesitation I lunge at him. Within seconds he is flailed open. Several other tribesmen rush at me with assorted weapons. The clubs do little, except to harden my scales as they strike. I dodge their attempts to stab me with wooden spears and swords as I sever heads and peel open their soft bodies.

I kill them all easily and suffer only one noticeable injury. A single slash from a blade has sliced open three of my scales. I examine the seeping wound carefully, then noting that the secondary scales are unharmed, leave it be. The damaged scales will flake off over the next few days, allowing new ones to grow into place.

I scrutinize one of the natives, and clearly see the man's small button nose, and tiny round ears. His narrow eyes are wide open, and dark, like pits. One member of the group has brown hair instead of the black the rest carry. A few of them have facial hair, which they seem to trim into differing shapes.

The sound of footfalls from behind, alerts me to the beast which is cautiously exiting my cave. The creature sniffs the air as it warily approaches me. It glances at the corpses, lifts its upper lip in a snarl, and then it plods toward me. I know the creature has little intelligence, but its instincts were spot on. It would seem these tribesmen were tracking it, and based on the animal skins they wear, use these creature's pelts for warmth.

The beast pads its way closer and closer to me, and then surprises me when it lays next to me. I retract my claws and stroke the soft fur on its back. The animal is behaving like a domesticated pet.

I mumble, "You are one mad cat!" Then, with a grin, I decide that I shall call it just that, Madcat. The animal purrs deeply as I continue to rub its fur.

Looking at the mess I have made, I realize that I had better eliminate the evidence of the massacre. I strip the bodies naked, burn their clothes, and store their weapons inside the main cave area. As for the bodies, I can think of no better use than as food for my new friend, and her brood.

By late afternoon the cats are well-fed. I take the remains to a nearby cave and bury them. Once done, I stare out at the valley and begin to consider the long-term ramifications of days like today.

Although I no longer require any more animal skins, I still kill a beast each day and prepare more dried meat. I share the spoils with Madcat and her growing young. The days pass quickly, as do the nights which I spend in my pod learning everything I can from the craft's computer. I have also discovered that I am an experimental version of my species. This knowledge intrigues me.

It seems that I am a generation five Mamluk and am expected to live for fifty cycles. Generation fives are sterile, and thus I am unable to reproduce. It seems that I, and others of my kind, are sent to planets as an advanced vanguard to wipe out the indigenous populations. Then, once we die off, cleanup teams collect our corpses, bury the bones of the dead, and then survey the planet for the colonial builders. However, I have a special designation next to my file, 'Generation 5.8.i'. The point eight, I understand as to mean that I am the eighth revision of my generation. But what is the 'i' for, I can find no references to it in the shuttle's computer.

I am still distracted by this curiosity as I exit my cave. I freeze, quickly tap Madcat's flank, and begin to retreat. A large group is establishing a camp between our cave and the creek. The growing, and playful, cubs dart outside, oblivious to the danger they have put all of us in. Madcat hisses at her young, but they continue to play, drawing attention to themselves in the process.

I shake my head as I decide whether to retreat into the cave, or to engage the campsite's inhabitants. A handful of well-armed men approach the cubs. They brandish an odd assortment of weapons. Some wield metal tipped spears, while others have bows. A clutch of men wearing leather jerkins and carrying a variety of swords, rushes toward the cubs. Madcat crouches to the ground with her ears flat against her head, and makes her intentions well known. I glance at the campsite which is still being set up. Dozens of men, women, and children are busy raising tents, while others gather water from the stream.

I sigh deeply. At this point there is no way I can avoid a conflict. I step into plain view and roar loudly. The men with swords skid and stumble as they attempt to stop. I kick off my makeshift shoes, and rush at them. My heel's rearward claws dig deeply into the ground as I sprint toward the armed men. I glance to my right and see Madcat keeping pace. The two of us quickly pass her cubs as we close the distance. The upcoming battle causes massive doses of adrenaline to kick in, hardening my scales to levels I have never experienced before.

An arrow unexpectedly flies past my head. I glance ahead, and then quickly block another that was aiming straight at my feline friend. The arrowhead strikes my arm, but does not penetrate my scales. I swat a handful of arrows from the air as we approach the leather clad swordsmen. I leap high into the air, and land in the midst of four men. I crouch down and raise my foot, with its rearward spike still fully extended, and sweep around in a full circle. All four men fall to the ground clutching at their torn open stomachs. Their leather tunics are no match for my powerful claws.

A group comes running at me, swinging their swords wildly. I stand and dodge their initial swings and stabs. I grab one of the men's arms, and jerk, instantly dislocating his shoulder. The man screams as he drops his sword. I ignore him for now, and face off against the growing number of attackers.

An arrow strikes my chest and pierces my scales. I stare at the arrow in disbelief as it wobbles back and forth. I pull it out and fling it to the ground angrily. My opponents begin to back away fearfully. Another arrow strikes me, but this one ricochets off my body. I glance to the man whose arm hangs uselessly, and grin when I see Madcat approaching him.

I turn to the group of twenty men, and then charge at them. I dodge swords, spears, and arrows, as I swipe at the first man I get to. My razor-sharp claws sever his head from his body in one swipe. A fountain of bright red blood gushes from his neck, spraying all those around him with its hot stickiness. The victim's headless form twitches involuntarily on the ground.

Another swings his sword at my midsection in a mighty blow. The sword lodges into my hardened scales but does not penetrate any deeper. The man frantically pulls on his sword, then as I grab his head, he defecates himself. I break his neck with one twist, then remove his sword from my side and throw it at another that is approaching Madcat. The sword strikes him, knocking him down.

I glance left and right, then decide that I have no time to waste. I sprint through the group of soldiers, slashing, goring, and gouging all I run past. A mountain of a man stands before me, beating on his chest. I stop, and without a second's hesitation ram my hand into his stomach. My extended claws impale him deeply. His eyes go wide as I drive my hand deeper into his ruined stomach. With his life fading from his eyes I tear his ribcage out from inside his body. I throw a handful of his broken and bloodied ribs at another man, and then dodge a spear which whisks past my head.

A high pitch scream greets my ears. Madcat is injured. I know that I should have no remorse or sympathy, but that does not stop me from discovering feelings that I never knew I had. I charge with a berserk rage at the man who has stabbed Madcat with his spear. The man strikes at the wounded cat again, but his spear never touches the animal. He stares at his severed arm with wide eyes, then staggers away clutching at the stump in a futile attempt to staunch the blood that spurts out with each beat of his heart.

I then stand over my wounded companion, and roar. Less than ten men stand before me, and some of those are clutching wounds. The men back away, then as a group, they flee. There is no point chasing them, others had already fled on the backs of riding animals the minute I charged at the main group.

I glance down at Madcat; she is laying on her side, panting. Blood drips from her nose. Her tan fur is matted with more, as it pours freely from a hole in her chest. I am surprised when she lets me examine the wound. It is deep, and has punctured one of her lungs, but the spear seems to have missed her heart. Turning my attention to the fleeing tribesmen and women, I can see that they are no longer a threat.

I stroke Madcat's head, then hoping the animal has the sense to stay put, hurry to my craft and get the medical kit. It takes me the better part of an hour to staunch the blood flow. She growls at me as I work to cauterize the wound, and then stitch it shut, but she lets me do so.

I carefully carry her back to the cave, where I lay her down on a couple of hides. Her young seem subdued, almost as if they know that they are the cause of their mother's plight. I stare at the animal and wonder about my own actions. Killing is what I was created to do, and yet here I am tending to a wounded animal. I glance at the entryway to my cave and wonder how long it will be before the locals come back in force.

For three days I tend to the injured cat, providing food and water as it lays on the animal skins. I spend much of this time burning the abandoned tents and piling up the dead. During this time, I formulate a plan, one that I am looking forward to carrying out.

I also realize that it would help me greatly if I could understand the native's language. The shuttle's computer is full of schematics on translators, but I do not have the tools, or parts, to make one. One of the images looks oddly familiar. Suddenly, I recall the items that were on the bodies of the pilots. I cast my gaze over the objects on the chair and grin. Sure enough, one is a translator. Why the man had one, I will probably never know. I follow the computer's instructions, turn it on, and then place the small unit in my ear. It was not designed for the shape of the inside of my ears and threatens to fall out. I take some wire that is encased in dark insulation, and then fashion a small frame. It takes some tweaking, but eventually I am happy with the way it sits. I shake my head, lift my ears up, and down, and the small unit remains in place. Now, to find a way to test it.

On the fourth day, I watch as Madcat rises and slowly pads her way outside. She has difficulty making her way up and over the pile of rocks to the partially concealed passageway. She manages, despite the fact that her cubs try to play with her. I doubt that she will ever fully recover from her injury. I just hope, that in time, she will be able to hunt for herself again. I follow the brood outside and smile as she makes her way to the stream, her young in tow.

The smell from the pile of corpses wafts in my direction from time to time, reminding me that I have a task to complete. I dig up the decomposing bodies of the shuttle's pilots and drag their remains outside on an animal skin. The pilots look similar to the locals, as in that they are both humanoid. However, the pilots have paler skin, less hair, and smaller heads. Their clothes are also obviously different. I find the smallest daggers, and place one in each of their hands. Then I arrange the corpses so that they form a ring around the two pilots, as if they fought to their death in the midst of an overwhelming force.

I stand back and survey the scene. I consider that those who fled will have stories of a strange creature with claws, and when they return, they will find a pair of aliens with daggers. Hopefully, this will make those who listen to the testimony of those who fled, doubt their story.

Next, I return to the cave where I hid the corpses from my previous engagement with the locals. I remove my makeshift footwear and pace around the cave, leaving massive paw prints. I then walk to and from the stream at least a dozen times, then finally I put my shoes back on and return to my cave.

As I reenter my cave, I debate whether I should make a doorway. I look around and decide that by leaving everything as it is, the cave appears to be no more than a den for a mother and her litter. I glance at the collection of weapons, and then move them into the concealed area with the shuttle. With everything in place, I wait, and continue to monitor Madcat's wound. It is healing, and thanks to the craft's medical supplies, there is no sign of infection.

I wake the next day and, as I step out of my pod, immediately hear Madcat's low growl. I hurry out of the shuttle, and over the makeshift wall. I then quietly make my way along the narrow passageway. I slowly peek outside, and then grin. A group of twenty or so heavily armed men, riding large four-legged animals, are following my tracks that lead to and from the other cave.

A pair of them ride in my direction. I retreat deeper into the darkness. One of the men dismounts and then walks into the narrow opening. He stares at the ground, and then says something unintelligible. The other man replies, and then rides away, to return a few minutes later with a lit torch. The flames flicker in the breeze, but do not go out. The man on foot takes the torch and then slowly walks inside. I stay well back, out of the range of his torch's flickering glow, and quietly retreat, keeping him in my sight. The intrepid torch wielder talks nonstop to the man outside. He crouches down and examines the tracks left by Madcat and her brood. He seems to ignore the large impressions left by my makeshift sandals.

The man makes his way to the bend, and then slowly walks around it. He holds his flaming torch well in front of him. He stops, stares at the rock walls, and then examines them more closely.

As I back up the slope, I dislodge a few small rocks, and cringe. The man jumps back in fright, and then shouts something that my earpiece is still unable translate. His colleague replies, and then the man with the torch begins to slowly back out of the passage.

The pair leave on their riding animals and join the group which is investigating the shuttle pilots' bodies. I am sure that their advanced state of decomposition is adding to the mystery. The group spends much of the remainder of the day scouting around, and finally they pile all the bodies in one place and burn them. The group then rides off.

The days come and go, and as they do the temperature slowly drops. Winter is coming to the region. Madcat's young grow fast and are now almost as large as their mother. She has recovered from her injury, except that she tires quickly when hunting food. My pod continues to operate, which amazes me. I continue to learn as much as I can during my sleep cycles. I am especially curious as to why I care for the feline.

During this time, I examine the objects that I left on the remaining pilot's chair. I feel a chill run up my spine when I realize that one of the items is a data clip. I activate the shuttle's pilot station and then review the information. I stagger back as the ramifications of what I read strike home.

I am an experimental version of my species, one designed for personal security. I was to be assigned to an individual, whom I was to protect at all costs. These pilots were transporting me to a secret facility for further testing and training prior to delivery. As the entire project is outside the scope of the Protectorate's primary mandate, only a few military commanders are even aware of my existence. That could explain why no one has come searching for me. It is hard to justify searching for something that officially does not exist.

The data clip's orders are quite specific. The project makes use of civilian transports, and special contractors, to disguise what they are really doing. There are other comments regarding the transfer of large sums of currency, which makes me wonder how legitimate my transport really was. The phrase, 'un-programmed unit', keeps appearing within the text numerous times.

Though I have a greater understanding of who I am, I still have no idea why I feel empathy for an animal. In fact, having feelings at all seems at odds with my function.

Suddenly my screen goes blank. I have just drained the shuttle's power to zero. The small solar panel will take a long time to recharge the craft. I walk back to my pod; it too is unpowered. I decide to sleep in it anyway, even though the training feature is offline.

I awake to the sound of Madcat growling loudly and am instantly alert. I rush out of the shuttle, and then cautiously peer over the top of the wall between the shuttle and the main cave area. There is no one in the cave, however there is an unusual sound coming from outside. A strange rumbling that seems to ebb and flow.

I make my way outside, to find it still dark. My eyes automatically revert to their thermal mode, and yet, I still cannot locate the source of the noise. I feel a faint vibration through the ground. Finally, in the distance, I can see a strange heat signature approaching from upstream. As the massive blob gets closer, I begin to make out individual shapes. It is a stampede!

Thousands of animals' rush down the valley. I can discern at least five different species of four legged animals, all freely running together. The sound the mass of animals makes intensifies as they get closer. Between their footfalls, and their various animal cries, the noise becomes deafening. The rumble of the thousands of hooves causes a minor landslide down the hill, causing me to retreat inside my cave.

The animals eventually pass, leaving behind an unusual and serene quietness. The morning's rays show the devastation the animals have left in their wake. The grass has not only been beaten down, but a trough now exists in the valley. One that stretches in both directions for as far as I can see.

I am curious about what caused the stampede and follow the downtrodden ground to its source. The trek takes me the better part of the day and leads me to a narrow valley between high mountain peaks. The air feels warmer, when it should be cooler. I stare up at small grey objects which float down from the sky. I am bewildered for a moment, and then it occurs to me, it looks like ash from a smoky fire.

I slowly make my way closer to the source, and then stare down into a massive crater. Lava bubbles in the hole and seems to be flowing. The longer I watch, the more it dawns on me that this is a lava tube, one where a section of its roof has caved in. Gazing at the countryside, I follow the contours of the hills, and visualize where the flow is travelling. It looks as though the valley with my cave is safe, which is a relief.

I return to my cave, to find Madcat pacing all over. She growls, then leads her grown cubs outside. I follow the brood back outside and watch as they leave. Once they disappear from sight, I turn to look in the direction of the lava tube, and wonder.

Winter

The days get shorter and cooler and although I sleep in the pod, I do not activate its training feature. Instead, I painstakingly watch the craft's energy levels slowly climb thanks to the small solar collector. Usually I do not require much rest or sleep, but with nothing to do, I find myself becoming more and more lethargic.

Light flurries of snow fall, peppering the grassland with white patches. As the days get shorter, the amount of snow increases, until the ground is almost completely covered. I step outside the cave one morning and stop and stare at the transformed landscape. Throughout the night, a lot of snow has fallen and covered the ground. I leave deep and distinctive tracks as I make my way to the creek. It still flows, though its edges are freezing over.

A cool wind blows down the valley, bringing with it more snowflakes. The wind gusts increase in frequency and intensity, blowing great billows of snow around. Fresh snow begins to fall from the sky as the wind howls down the valley. I retreat to my cave and am most relieved when I finally clamber inside the protective walls. I watch as the snow gets deeper and deeper, eventually covering the entrance to my cave completely.

I have learned that the transport has a crude tool kit. Inside is a multi-tool, with which I remove the door between the cockpit and the rear section which houses the pods. It takes four days to carve the door into pieces, and then put these together to cover the hole in the front. The multi-tool is not designed for large projects and requires recharging each night. This tool requires a lot of energy, and noticeably drains the craft's limited reserve. I notice the power levels drop below five percent, and do not climb, indicating that the solar panel is so deeply covered in snow, that it is now useless.

I stare at the sealed window with a sense of pride. If the solar collector still works when the snow melts, I will be able to pressure test the inside of the ship. With nothing else to do, I retire to my inactive pod, and sleep.

Chapter Two - Discovered

I wake and am instantly alarmed. Cobwebs crisscross their way across the opening to my pod. My eyes feel dry, and my joints feel stiff. I brush away the cobwebs as I hurriedly step out. The craft's energy levels are alarmingly low. Three percent! I glance at the dust covered panels once more and frown. According to the terminal, I have been asleep for months.

I drink deeply from the stores of water, and then eat a sparing amount of the food strips I had prepared. I cautiously make my way outside, where I am greeted by a morning sun. I climb the hill and examine the solar panel. I dust it off, and smile. It has survived the winter and continues to provide a trickle of power to the transport.

I make my way back to the craft and immediately research all I can about my extended sleep. Discovering that this is normal for my species, relieves me. It seems that when my species has no instructions, and is not in any danger, we hibernate. This extends our life expectance beyond the fifty cycles I had thought we lived. We have fifty cycles of active time.

I then investigate why I lost power when everything was off. I stare in disbelief at the results, and mentally kick myself. The solar panel is part of the distress beacon, and when the unit was unable to power itself, it automatically drew from the craft's reserves. Fortunately, I had disconnected the transmitter, but that did not stop the beacon from draining power, regardless.

I shut down the craft's power, and then return to the solar panel. I examine the unit, trying to figure out how to disable the power drain. I stare at the circuit board and then sigh. Its features appear to be fully integrated, thus I am reluctant to mess with it.

My hunger and frustration combine and build up inside me. I stand and loudly roar across the valley. Staring down at the four-legged creatures grazing in the grass covered valley fills me with bloodlust. I sprint down the hill, and charge at a group of these animals. The creatures flee the second they sense danger, but I am faster. With a single swipe of my clawed hand, I bring one down, almost cleaving its head from its body. I feel a strange euphoria and kill three more beasts before my desire to kill is sated.

I build a large fire near the creek, and slow roast them all. I am enjoying my feast when a beast with tan fur comes into view. I stare at the cat-like animal, then notice a familiar scar on its chest. "Madcat, you're back!" I shout excitedly.

The animal pads its way to my side, then lays down. I rub its belly and feel a strange sense of satisfaction in doing do. The creature makes strange noises as I stroke its fur.

Once the fire is mere ashes, Madcat rolls onto her four paws and approaches the carcasses. She rips huge chunks of meat off the roasted animals with her powerful jaws. She eats her fill, and then makes her way to my cave. I stare at the embers, and then decide to retire to my pod. I activate the training program, searching for ways to increase my power build up, and then sleep.

I spend the next few days searching the caves for a quartz-like material that the shuttle's computer has indicated to exist. Apparently, the crystals will enhance the solar panel's collection rate. I strategically place each one I find around the solar collector. I direct as much sunlight as is possible to the unit, while preventing any tell-tale glow from being visible. This is much more difficult than I first thought it would be. Finally, I am confident that any glint or glow from the crystals is not visible from the ridgeline above, or the valley below.

I increase my stock of dried meat and refill my water storage unit. I stare at the full indicator on the reservoir and suddenly realize that this is yet another passive system that requires power. I frown as it dawns on me that having actual water, and not a synthetic form from a food processor, is extremely inefficient. I immediately begin to research this, and once again it comes down to the way my kind is transported. When deposited on planets to perform our killing sprees, we are left with an initial supply of water.

A few days later, I am drying and preparing more food strips, when I look up and see a figure standing on the hilltop's ridgeline. The tribesman is watching me, seemingly studying me. I do not know how long the person has been there, but my failure to notice the man sooner alarms me. He carries a long pole, which he uses to assist his steps as he retreats out of sight.

I immediately sprint toward the top of the ridge. The hillside is steep, and in my haste, I use all fours to speed up my climb. I arrive at the top, almost breathless, and stop in my tracks at what I see. Hundreds of men are below, sitting astride animals. They seem to be waiting for something. One of the men lifts an object to his mouth. The horn bellows deeply and loudly, echoing up and down the valley.

A chill works its way up my spine when I realize that not all the sounds are echoes. Another horn sounds from the bottom of the valley. I spin around in alarm at the sound of yet another coming from my valley. A troop of heavily armed men are riding toward my cave. I grimace, and then look at the only direction left open to me, the mountains where I discovered the lava tube.

I run!

I stick to the top of the mountain ridge, making sure that both sides can easily see me. I smile when I see both sets of riders following me; Madcat will be left alone. I maintain a brisk pace, while constantly scanning the area ahead. The valleys on either side slope upward, while the ridgeline does not, meaning that soon enough I will be at the same level as those following me. I know the pursuers think that I am being driven into their trap. But the key to avoiding a trap, is knowing one exists. I narrow my eyes and then spot what I am looking for. Far in the distance are groups of men, all crouching down behind a series of low rock walls.

My muscles begin to ache, and my breath begins to labor, causing me to slow down. This seems to give my pursuers additional incentive to close the distance. I hear them shouting at their animals, encouraging them to run faster. The groups begin to string out as some gallop faster than others. I glance to my right, measuring the forces, and then redoubling my efforts, sprint along the ridge top.

I see an opportunity and take it. I hurtle down the left-hand side of the mountain, straight at the leading elements of the riders. They do not stand a chance. The men dismount and seize their weapons as I approach. Eight men face me, all brandishing swords and knives. More than a hundred of their kind are riding toward me, but the unlucky souls before me, rode ahead of the main group, and will now pay for their arrogance.

I let them come at me. They slash, stab, and swing their weapons wildly. I dodge, and swipe in return. I rip one open from his throat to his sternum, another I strike so hard, his head falls back, held in place by a few tendons and a patch of skin. Another man lunges at me, and misses. I wrench his arm so hard I can hear, and feel, as something tears in his shoulder. He screams as he clutches his ruined arm.

A brute of a man screams incoherently while he swings an axe down at my head. I deflect the blow, driving the axe down, and then swing it back up at the man. He stares at me in shock as the axe head buries its way into his groin. He falls to the ground, while trying to hold his entrails in place as they snake out from his body.

Another group of riders' approach, but these men remain mounted. They too pay for their mistake. With one huge swipe, I break the legs of their animals, toppling the hapless riders to the ground where I dispatch them quickly.

Blood runs freely down my arms and chest, but it is not my blood that flows. Three more men cautiously approach, their swords pointed at me menacingly. They shout and charge as one. I jump upward with all my might. Landing on the back of one of the men, my weight drives him to the ground. I then stomp on the back of his head; my rearward claw cleaves his skull. Striding to the remaining men, they stare fearfully at my foot, as their colleague's brains drip from it.

With another group of riders approaching, both men regain their confidence, and stab at me. I twist and turn, narrowly dodging both blades. I grab both of their heads, and then crack them together. The noise of their skulls shattering causes the remaining riders to turn and flee.

I stare euphorically at the blood-stained grass, my adrenaline and blood lust increasing with each encounter.

Turning at the sound of hoof beats, I see thirty or so riders have regrouped and are bearing down on me. I roar at them loudly, then turn and flee once more; easily avoiding the men hiding behind the rocks as I make my way to the lava. The pursuers stay together; no one it seems wants to get to me first.

I arrive at the collapsed lava tube, and grin when I see that another section has caved in, exposing more of the hot bubbling liquid. I position myself behind the collapsed sections and wait. I do not have to wait long. It is not fear or anxiety that I feel when I see that the number of riders is in the hundreds, but I am definitely experiencing an odd sensation. Where the extra forces came from, I have no idea. They ride at me in reckless abandon, then seeing the lava, many of them dismount. Others ride off, undoubtedly in an attempt to flank my position.

I stand my ground as the first wave of men charges at me, their swords flashing in the sunlight. I dodge left and right, then lunge forward, striking two of them down with one slash of my claws. I jump back, narrowly avoiding a massive sword. It swings down and strikes the ground with a resounding clang. I lift my foot and spin around. My rear claw slashes across the swordsman's throat, spurting hot blood all over my leg and the ground.

I jump back as another sword swings at me. The man screams at me incoherently, either to frighten me, or to bolster his own courage. In either case, his efforts are wasted. I cleave his head from his body with such force that it spins over and over in the air. His body topples to the ground and twitches. The stump of his neck pumps out volumes of blood in seconds. The man's mouth is still open when his skull thumps to the ground. His eyes seem to grimace at the impact, and even try to focus as his head rolls to a stop.

I whirl at the sound of hoof beats. A group of fifteen riders sit atop their beasts, blocking my path. A spear hurtles past my shoulder from behind and strikes the rocks nearby. I stare at the riders, and then turn my attention to the spear thrower. Twenty men slowly approach me; each is armed with a sword or sharpened pole. I retrieve the spear that was thrown at me, and then swing it around in a wide arc, keeping my attackers at bay.

They rush at me, swords and spears alike come at me in overwhelming numbers. I charge at the group of men, pushing and shoving them back, until they fall into the open lava tube. Their screams and cries are cut off quickly as the searing heat burns them alive. I grab a spear that is thrust at me, and then twist. The hapless man holds on tightly, and does not let go, even as I shove him closer to the open lava tube. He loses his footing and falls into the bubbling lava. His screams echo loudly as he burns.

I lose count of how many I kill before something strikes the back of my head. I stagger as

I struggle to remain standing, but blackness overcomes me as my consciousness escapes.

I shake my head as I come to. A dull ache throbs through my head and shoulders. I attempt to move my hands, but only succeed in causing a shooting pain to run through my body. I look down and see two long spears sticking out from my upper chest. My arms and legs are tied to a massive tree trunk. I can feel blood seeping down my back, telling me that the spears have been run straight through, pinning me to the tree. I stare at my captors, counting twenty-seven men. I hear others behind me, perhaps as many as ten more.

A man approaches carrying a dagger. He pries open a scale on my chest, then peels it off. The pain is minimal, and easily ignored. He pokes at the softer, and more sensitive secondary scales beneath, with the tip of his dagger. I resist the urge to flinch, but my injuries make this difficult.

The man smiles at my discomfort, then turns to another and says, "Why did you want to catch this creature alive?"

A man dressed in ornate armor steps into view and replies, "This creature has been observed cooking food, and preparing animal skins. I want to know where it is from. Is this thing a random aberration, or are there more of his kind?"

"I am alone." I reply as I gather my wits.

The men jump back in fear. The translator has not only been able to acquire their language, but thanks to its advanced architecture, I am also able to converse with them.

The ornately dressed man, who is clearly their leader, regains his composure and demands, "Why did you attack my people?"

"Attack you?" I reply in disbelief. I then state venomously, "Your kind attacked me first!"

"Where are you from?" The man demands, ignoring my comment.

I glance upward as I reply, "The stars!"

The man draws his sword, and then presses the tip between two scales as he hotly demands, "Why are you here? What do you want?"

"I crashed, and as for what I want. I wish to be left alone, until I can depart your backward world." I stare at the man, ignoring the pain as he pushes the tip of his sword into my stomach. I can feel it tearing my scales, and then sliding inside.

The man withdraws his sword, and then holds the bloody tip high as he shouts, "The demon from the sky bleeds! It can be defeated."

I consider the blood that freely runs down my chest and back and wonder what the symbolism is for. As it is obvious that I bleed. I know what I must do if I am to escape and take a deep breath.

The leader whirls around and strikes. His sword lodges deeply into the tree. However, I am no longer bound to it, instead I stare down at him from an overhead branch. I drop to the ground, striking downward with one of the two spears that had held me in place. The tip of the spear easily penetrates the man's shoulder. I drive the shaft down as I land on the ground, until the tip exits his lower back. He coughs great gouts of blood, and then falls to the ground.

I roar loudly at his men and smile as I watch them run away as fast as their legs can carry them. As soon as the last of them has fled, I examine my injuries. I will need to get to my pod, and soon, if I am to survive. I hope that its deep-sleep function will allow my body to heal. Glancing down, I notice that the impaled man is wearing my belt, which I retrieve. I quickly examine its contents and am surprised to find everything is there.

I stare at the foliage overhead, and then being unable to determine where I am, walk off in a random direction.

Reflecting on my escape, I smile. Cutting the ropes was easy, the edges of my scales slowly worked their way through the rope's strands. Ripping the spears from my body took effort. Fortunately, the only place they could drive them through has no major organs. My muscle fibers will heal, in time, but I must staunch the blood flow. It dribbles down my chest and back with each exertion.

As soon as I feel it is safe, I stop and build a fire. I crudely cauterize my wounds, and then depart, leaving the burning fire. As night falls, I am able to see a few stars, and begin to get my bearings. I realize that I must have been unconscious for quite some time. Somehow, I have been transported away from the lava, and into a forest area downstream from my cave.

I adjust my heading, and laboriously continue walking. Sunlight begin to peek over the horizon as the valley with my cave comes into view. My mouth is dry, and my muscles quiver with each fresh exertion. I fall to the ground and lay there for a moment. My wounds have begun bleeding again, sapping what remains of my strength.

I open my eyes, startled and alarmed. Something is licking my face. I turn my head and stare into the eyes of a large predator. "Madcat," I utter softly, "it's you." I lay my head down, instantly relieved.

I awake to a strange tugging sensation in my arm. The cat-like animal is dragging me. Its mouth gripping my wrist with just enough force to hold me, without tearing my scales. The animal lets my hand go, and then crouches next to me.

I pet my loyal friend, and then summon all of my strength. I am unable to stand, so instead I crawl toward the creek. It takes me a while to get there, but as soon as I do, I plunge my head into the cool waters. I drink deeply, and then lay on the grass.

A deep low growl from Madcat alarms me. I flop onto my back and stare into the distance. With difficulty I focus on a solitary figure that approaches. The approaching man draws out a sword as he gets closer. Madcat jumps away, and lands between the stranger and me. The man does not call out and would seem to be alone. He swings his sword at my protector, and then curses when he misses.

The man lunges, and stabs viciously at Madcat. His confidence is also his downfall. I watch with fascination as Madcat leaps up, and over the man. At the apex of her flight she swipes at the man's head. The man falls to the ground, clutching at a series of deep gouges in his scalp. His body twitches and spasms, his brains seeping from the open wounds.

With difficulty, I crawl toward Madcat, and then cling to the animal's fur, allowing my savior to drag me. I am weak from blood loss and assist as best I can. It takes quite a while, but eventually we arrive at my cave.

It is a struggle to climb the wall and get to my shuttle. The medical kit still has the supplies I need, and with it, I patch up my injuries as best as I can. I stare at the craft's energy supply and cringe. It will take most, if not all, of the available power to run my pod. Adding to my woes, I look up and notice that my makeshift repairs have failed. Massive cracks occupy the area where the modified door meets the window frame. I will have to fix this another time.

I eat copious amounts of my supplies of dried meat, and then take what I have left and give it to Madcat. She sniffs at my offerings but seems unimpressed with the preserved meat.

While petting and stroking the animal's fur, I softly explain. "I have to sleep, and let my wounds heal. I have no idea how long your species lives, so I do not know if I will see you again my friend." Madcat purrs, and then as I step away, she falls to sleep on the floor of my cave. I know the animal cannot understand me, and yet I feel as if somehow, she does.

With a reluctant sigh I engage my pod's deep-sleep mode and enter it. As soon as the cover panel slides shut, I fall into a coma-like state. The craft's training system continues to function and provides me with more knowledge than I ever thought possible.

Sanctuary

I wake up just as the pod's covering is sliding back. My throat is dry, and my stomach rumbles in hunger. I eat and drink from my stores and check my wounds. As I had hoped, the pod's deep-sleep function allowed my body to heal. My damaged scales have flaked off, leaving no outward sign of my injuries.

I step into the cockpit area and wipe a thin layer of dust off the craft's control panels. I stare at the large cracks where I attempted to seal the window and decide that I will have to remove the panel and start from scratch.

I have slumbered through an entire century, give or take a few years. As I feared, the craft's power reserve is nearly depleted. Sighing heavily, I wonder if I will ever escape this planet. I run the ship's systems through a complete diagnostic routine, and even fire up each of the thrusters for a few seconds. The cave quickly fills with dust, confirming that they are all still functional. Having used up all the remaining reserves, I shut down the shuttle's systems and then look to my pod and wonder how it was able to remain functional. According to my readings, the solar panels stopped providing any practical value long ago. I go to one of the unused pods, open its rear casing, and discover a small independent power unit.

I look at the four pods and realize that I should have known they would have their own backup systems. I make my way to the entrance to discover that it is blocked by rocks. I carefully clear the way, and then step outside. The daylight is blindingly bright. Once my eyes adjust, and I can see clearly, I gaze around. The sun is high overhead casting its rays across the lush grasslands and the four-legged animals that are grazing. The nearby creek flows faster and has eroded a slightly different path through the meadow than I recall. I frown as I turn to look at the distant hills where the lava tubes should be. The area is shrouded in a grey ash cloud. It would seem that the lava is becoming more active.

I turn and make my way up the hill to the solar collector. Finding that it appears undamaged pleases me. I carefully clear its surface of dust and dirt. I find the crystals that I had arranged around the unit, then clean and reposition them. Next, I climb to the top of the mountain, and take in the view. Following the valleys downstream, I can see smoke rising in the distance. The tendrils of smoke appear to be localized, perhaps from an encampment, or a small town.

Feeling energized, and curious, I decide to see how much this civilization has developed during my slumber. I keep a sharp lookout for any of the local inhabitants, especially after my last encounter. The distant forest, in which I was pinned to a tree, is much sparser than I recall. As I get closer, I notice tree stumps in the woods. Examining one shows that it was chopped down, and the tree's trunk taken away. Edging my way through the thin woodlands, I come upon its fringe, and stop. Before me rests a small town, its dozens of wooden dwellings form a crude circle around a huge central courtyard. Beasts of burden haul wagons, while others carry townsfolk. Staying hidden amongst the trees, I make my way around the town, scrutinizing it. Two dirt roads lead out of the area, neither of which heads toward my valley and cave. A crude, yet wide, trail leads to the fast-flowing stream. Most of the buildings are single story, though a couple of the larger ones are two story, with wide balconies. I observe the inhabitants exchanging goods for currency and pay special attention to the fact that none of them appears to be armed.

Nodding appreciatively at their progress, I head back to my cave. Although the inhabitants have little in the way of technology, the social levels required to maintain a peaceful township indicate a centralized government.

Upon my return I review the craft's power reserve. I sigh at the trickle of energy that is coming in from the solar panel. I turn my attentions to my food and water and decide to build up my stocks. My first task is to figure out a way to prepare new food cubes, using the local animal life and the craft's small food reprocessor.

Suddenly it dawns on me, I have, at my disposal, the means to eliminate all my problems. The tool I used to repair the hull breach can manufacture just about any basic object. I gaze around and then see what I am looking for. The three pods I am not using, all have curved, metallic coverings which slide into place. I slowly dismantle one, and then begin preparing its inside surface. I create a series of small solar panels inside the reflective curved area. Once done, I carry it outside and up to my existing collector. I dig a depression, and carefully rest my creation in the hole, and then place rocks around it. Lastly, I connect the solar beacon to my invention, and then wait. When nothing unusual happens, I hurry to the transport and check the charge indicator. I jump around excitedly, shouting, "It works!"

I spend the next few days adding more makeshift panels, turning the trickle of energy into something more reasonable. During this time, I wonder about Madcat and her brood. I have not seen any sign of her, or others of her kind, as I labored.

I open my eyes and exit my pod. I pause mid-breath and scowl. An all too familiar odor assaults my nose. Making my way over the makeshift wall, I stop as soon as I spot the man. He is standing in the middle of my cave with his hands held high in the air. At his feet is a small campfire, its flames create flickering shadows on the walls.

"I know you can understand me." The man states with confidence as he turns around and around; he must have heard me, but as of yet cannot see me.

I sit on my haunches and wait to see what the man does next.

He continues slowly turning around as he loudly announces, "My grandfather told us all about you, even when the King denied your existence, my grandfather continued to speak. He was one of the Royal Guards who captured you, you know. Well, I've been searching for you for a long time."

"Why?" I demand as I stand.

The man flinches when his eyes fall upon my form. He stammers, "At first, I only wanted to clear my family name, but now I want revenge." He turns his gaze and looks straight at me as he makes his plea, "If I can find you, so can others. In exchange for a safe haven, I will need your help in overthrowing my corrupt government and returning me to my rightful place."

I shake my head as I reply, "I have no need for your help, and no desire to assist you in your quest." I slowly make my way towards the man.

He keeps his hands up defensively and cries out fearfully, "Wait! My name is Jerry, and I really can help you."

I stop walking, and demand, "How?"

Jerry licks his lips nervously, then says, "Hunting parties search these hills every year, hoping to find and kill the beast of the mountains. They will eventually find you."

I tilt my head as I bluntly state, "I could just kill you now, and seal up the cave entrance."

"Yes, but they will eventually find that thing you're building on the hillside."

I stalk menacingly toward the man, grab his neck, and lift him off the ground. "How long have you been watching me?" I demand.

"Ugh!" Jerry's feet shake and twitch, while his arms flail about uselessly.

Jerry's vocal cords move beneath my hand, while his face turns red as my crushing grip saps his life. I stare at the fear in his eyes, and then lower him to the ground. The second I let him go he falls to his knees and gasps deep breaths of air. I smell an unusual odor, and then realize that the man has wet himself. I leave him, stride outside and stare at my surroundings.

Jerry staggers out from the cave, leaning on the rocks for support, and hoarsely speaks, "You can trust me. I could have gone to the authorities and told them of you, but instead I came alone, and unarmed."

I stare at the Jerry's deep blue eyes and state, "You only came because you thought you could use me to benefit your cause."

"Yes, that is true." He replies slowly, while rubbing his neck. He nervously stares at me as he speaks once more, "But, I really can offer you sanctuary."

I stare at the man and realize that his comments about being discovered have an element of truth to them. I turn to the cave as I ponder my situation. Trusting this man, Jerry, goes against my base instincts. But I have learned more from the pod's training database than my kind was ever intended to, which provides me with a unique perspective.

I spin around and point menacingly at the man as I spit out my threat, "If you attempt to deceive me, I will kill you, your family, and everyone you have ever known."

Jerry gulps, lowers his gaze, and then replies feebly, "You will help me then?"

"What is it you wish for me to do, exactly?" I respond.

His face twitches as he replies, "Kill the King, which will allow his daughter to marry me."

I roar with laughter at his ridiculous request. Jerry fretfully shifts his weight from one foot to the other as I weigh his requests. I shake my head at the man as I reply, "You are either a fool, or the bravest individual on this measly planet."

Jerry glances around and swallows hard as he says, "Does that mean you will help?"

I step closer to him and run a claw from his stomach to his neck as I sternly warn, "Remember, if you betray me, you and all you know, will die, slowly and painfully."

Jerry's head bobs up and down in quick jerking motions. He licks his lips as he responds, "I understand."

"Good." I reply, "Now help me seal my cave's entrance."

The two of us spend much of the day closing off the cave entrance. During this time, I take the medical kit and spread the various pieces throughout my pouches. I stand back, satisfied with our labors. Reopening the cave will take considerable effort, but then, that is my intention.

I turn to the Jerry and state, "Lead the way."

Jerry nods his head in nervous jerky motions, and then heads toward the creek. I follow the man across the narrow waterway, constantly alert to a trap. As we walk, I consider my main motive for following the man; I want to see who else knows of my existence. We cross the stream, skirt around the edge of a wooded area, and then begin to traverse a vast field.

Casting long shadows on the ground as we travel, Jerry surprisingly picks up the pace, even though he is clearly tiring. He gains a little confidence and begins to ramble. "Thanks to your escape from the Royal Guard, my grandfather was shamed, and exiled. Now our family lives on the foothills of the mountains ahead with a small group of loyal followers. Our king's entire family is mad; they kill or exile anyone who disagrees with them. The ruling family is insanely jealous of our powerful neighbors and wants to declare war on them all. But they can't, which frustrates them even more."

I sigh deeply as the man prattles on. I am not concerned with the petty problems of this backward world. Still, I take in his commentary, boring as it is.

Jerry glances back from time to time, even as his voice drones on, "If the King would open trade negotiations, we could have the same things the rich kingdoms do. That would… Ah!" He exclaims fearfully, stops, and points with a shaking finger ahead.

I shove Jerry to one side and step past him. Gazing ahead I am stunned at the sight before me. Madcat is slowly limping her way toward us. She looks old, her fur is thin, and her body gaunt, but her eyes still shine with vitality.

I smile as I walk toward the animal. Upon reaching her, I stroke her head and speak softly, "I did not think that you would still be alive, my old friend."

Jerry's shaky voice disturbs my unexpected melancholy, "You know this animal?" He asks incredulously.

"Yes," I reply, and then add bluntly, "and she is coming with us."

"Uh, no, that's not possible. They're dangerous and should be killed." Jerry responds.

I spin around and bluntly state, "Madcat comes with us! I will care for her. Besides, look at her; she is too old to be a threat to your people."

Jerry lowers his gaze, replying submissively, "As you wish."

Examining Madcat carefully, reveals that she is malnourished. "We're camping here," I inform Jerry, and then add, "I need to provide fresh food for her."

I do not wait for a reply and sprint off toward a distant herd of grazing animals. Returning with my spoils, Jerry has made himself useful, and has small fire going in a pit. Thin wisps of smoke drift up into the darkening skies, blending into the evening haze. As the last rays of the sun pass beyond the mountains, Jerry relaxes once more.

Madcat has always seemed intuitive, and today is no exception, for she has remained where I left her. I tear off chunks of raw meat from my kill and feed them to her. Her fur is so thin I can clearly make out the scar in her chest.

Jerry watches me warily; he is clearly baffled by my concern for the wild animal. Eventually he builds up the courage to ask, "I just saw you kill that harmless animal without a second's hesitation, and I know you have killed many of my kind. So, why not just put this dangerous beast out of its misery?"

I stroke Madcat's fur as I reply, "This creature saved my life, a debt I shall now repay."

Jerry accepts my statement with a nod of his head, and sits on the far side of the fire, away from us.

I turn to Jerry and ask, "Tell me more of your family, and why the King's daughter would marry you."

Jerry takes a deep breath, and then begins. "When you killed the guardsman and escaped, my grandfather was blamed. For his punishment, he was banished, which paved the way for the old King to establish his bastard son as the new rightful heir. My grandfather built a small villa in the foothills, with a few followers, and has been left alone since."

"And?" I prompt, becoming intrigued by Jerry's story.

Jerry continues, "The old king died, and the son immediately took power. The Royal Guard were all loyal to the new king, so when he ordered that my grandfather be put to death, they obeyed. Only four people escaped that night with their lives. My pregnant mother, and three faithful servants. The new King was concerned that my family's influence would rise once more to threaten his position."

I glance at Jerry as I comment, "So, your mother was pregnant with you, making you the only surviving male heir of his lineage."

"Yes," Jerry replies excitedly, "and in accordance with our kingdom's laws, I am the true heir to the throne. If the bastard son were to die, the council of elders would have little choice but to approve my crowning."

I shake my head as I ask, "How can you prove your linage?"

Jerry grins as he replies, "I have my grandfather's Royal Signet."

"A ring is all you need to prove your linage?" I ask doubtfully.

"It's not just a ring," Jerry states proudly, "it's my grandfather's Royal Seal."

"You still have not said why the daughter would marry you." I press.

"Oh," Jerry stalls, and then slowly admits, "she wants to."

When he offers no further explanation, I stare at him as I consider how archaic this world is. I then wonder how long it will be before I can escape.

As I ponder Jerry's comments the fire diminishes to smoldering embers, causing clouds of smoke to rise into the starry sky.

"Crap!" Jerry exclaims. He jumps up and covers the fire, sending one last blast of smoke into the sky before it is extinguished. "Night patrols are rare, but if there are any, the smoke would attract them."

I stare at the dissipating cloud that rises above, and then intently scan all around with my night vision. Once satisfied that the area is clear, I state, "There is no one."

"Okay," Jerry replies, a hint of skepticism entering his voice.

I pretend to sleep during the night, but remain vigilant of Jerry, and my surroundings. Madcat sleeps fitfully throughout the night; her body twitches, accompanied by an occasional groan.

The early rays of the sunrise peek over the distant mountains, reminding me of where we are headed. I tear off a great chunk of meat, and feed it to Madcat, which she gobbles down. She limps less this morning, which pleases me greatly. We move out, and initially make good time, but that soon changes.

Jerry sighs heavily as we stop once more. He looks around nervously and asks anxiously, "Can't your pet go any faster?"

"Nope!" I reply as I sit in the tall grass next to Madcat.

Jerry runs his fingers through his hair as he paces back and forth in exasperation. "But we have to return soon!" He states adamantly.

"Why the hurry?" I ask.

"It's not safe out here between the mountains. Especially at this time of the day. This area is the borderland between kingdoms, and both sides patrol this region." Jerry stares fearfully around, as if a great force were about to come crashing through the grassland at any moment.

I sigh, and begrudgingly turn my attention to the distant tree line we left behind us earlier in the morning. I am about to scold Jerry when I observe motion in the woods.

"Get down!" I hiss as I flop onto my stomach.

Jerry immediately falls to the ground and lays flat. He is quivering with fear.

I watch through the grass as the distant group casually walks through the woods. Their armor and weapons would seem to confirm Jerry's claim that this area is patrolled by military forces. After what feels like an eternity, the patrol turns and walks back the way they came.

Once they are out of sight, I state, "Jerry, keep low. We're moving out."

I keep a watchful eye behind us as we slowly make our way across the tundra. Madcat's pronounced limp sets a good pace as we cautiously move through the grass. It is late afternoon by the time we are close to the foothills of our destination.

Jerry stops, and declares, "We are close to where I live, and safe now."

I take stock of the foothills, and then smile. The grassland, woods, and creek form a natural border. Any invading forces would be seen long before they could traverse the distance.

"So, let me get this straight." I state, staring intently at Jerry, "All I need to do is to kill the King; you will become the next ruler and marry his daughter."

Jerry nods excitedly.

"That won't work!" I state bluntly.

Jerry's expression freezes on his face as he stammers, "Why not?"

I shake my head as I respond, "If it was that simple, you would have found a way to kill him."

"Uh, well," Jerry stammers, "one of the new laws is that if a successor assassinates the ruler, he is automatically denied the throne. The Royal Guard is sworn to uphold this law."

I grin as I finally understand Jerry's plan. "But if the beast from the mountains returns, and publicly kills him, with lots of witnesses, then you would simply be coming out of hiding to claim the throne."

"Exactly!" Jerry states excitedly, "Then you are seen fleeing to the lava pools where you fled to many years ago, confirming the rumors that you live there."

"I see," I continue, "and then I am supposed to simply return, and you will provide a safe haven."

Jerry slowly nods as he realizes that he has no way to prove that he can be trusted. He gulps, carefully removes his signet ring and says, "I am staking my entire future on this plan. Take my ring as proof of my intentions. I will need it to claim the throne."

I am surprised by his unexpected offer. It dawns on me that this man is serious and has a level of commitment that I had not anticipated. I take the ring and secure it inside a pouch on my belt.

We continue walking until we come upon the base of a massive hill. A wide, and well-travelled path leads up the side of the hill. Instead of slowing down, Jerry's pace picks up as we ascend. My claws click and clack as the dirt gives way to stone.

We arrive at a small village to be met by a handful of people, which soon turns into a small group. They hang back in fear, Madcat's growls clearly adding to their discomfort.

Jerry stops and puts his hands in the air as he addresses them in a loud, firm, voice, "Do not fear, these are my friends," he pauses as he realizes that he does not even know my name. He glances at me, then continues, "The creature I have been searching for is here to help us, in exchange for safety."

"What of that predator?" A voice demands from the crowd as he points venomously at Madcat.

I stretch to my full height and bellow, "I am Mamluk; Madcat is my faithful companion. If any harm comes to her, you all die!"

"And you expect us to trust you?" The same voice demands hotly.

"Yes," I bellow, "you can trust that if you hold to the bargain Jerry and I have struck, you will live, otherwise you will not."

Jerry waves his hands at the group and says, "Please, everyone relax. Everything we know of Mamluk is lies. We have talked at length, and he is an intelligent creature, not some mindless beast. Besides, he could have killed me anytime, but instead chose to accept my offer and come here."

Gazing at the group, I count fifteen people in all. Nine men, five women, and one child. The men wear leather jerkins and carry swords; the tattered dresses worn by the women give testimony to their bleak lifestyle. I stare at the child, a scruffy looking boy with his hands in his trouser pockets. He meets my gaze with a mixture of fear and curiosity. He smiles, and then waves excitedly at me. I grin back, causing the boy to gasp and then flee. I glance at the clutch of buildings and notice a few more people peering fearfully from behind curtained windows.

Jerry leads the way to a large villa, where he proudly states, "I have prepared an underground area for you; it has everything you could need."

I stare at the three-story villa, and in particular the balcony on its second level, then respond, "I will not be trapped underground. I will take that level."

Jerry's mouth opens to reply, but he remains silent. It takes the rest of the day to move Jerry's things out of the villa's second level, and to secure the doors leading to the stairways.

Madcat pads around the four rooms and shows her approval by climbing onto a bed in one of the rooms where she falls asleep. Looking at the massive predator sleeping on a bed is comical. Her head is even resting on a pillow, adding to the strange scene.

I decide to lay on another bed and find it surprisingly comfortable. I lay still for a moment and listen to the sounds around me. Leather soles strike the cobble stones as people walk the streets below. Quiet whispers come to my sensitive hearing; the locals are afraid. Angry shouts in the distance rise and fall as the town's discord ebbs and flows like the tide. Clearly my presence is not supported by all.

Instead of sleeping, I rise from the bed and use the crafting tool to build a small solar panel. The complex task of constructing a charger for the tool takes most of the evening. I find a suitable location on the balcony, one that will hopefully capture the sun's rays from dawn to dusk. With the crafting tool's charge being almost spent, I retire to the bed and rest.

The next few days are a blur. I spend most of my time enhancing the security on my level of the villa. I line the inside of the wooden doors with a thin layer of bioduropoly, the same material which coats the hull of most spacecraft. The substance is capable of self-repairing and, due to its molecular structure, is flexible while being almost impervious to penetration. I fashion crude weapons, and strategically place them around the entire villa. Providing food for Madcat is a problem, the local folk have no interest in giving up their meat, and yet when I attempt to hunt, Jerry advises that the less I go out, the less chance a distant patrol will spot me. I finally strike a bargain, whereby I go out with a hunting party and kill a beast or two each day. This provides the kitchen staff with an abundance of meat, some of which they prepare for Madcat. This system works well, and keeps most people happy, or at the very least content. The hunting parties are initially afraid of me, but soon begin to appreciate my ability at bringing down the local herbivores.

I awake early, as I usually do, and find Jerry waiting for me. I instantly wonder how he got into my room, and then realize that I have been getting lax with my own security.

Jerry gazes down at his feet as he quietly speaks, "We have an opportunity to kill the King."

"Elaborate," I reply bluntly.

He takes a deep breath, and then begins, "The King will be travelling from his home castle to another on the far side of our kingdom. The Royal Guard, which currently numbers some one hundred soldiers, is his usual escort."

"When do they leave?"

"In three days!" Jerry replies hesitantly.

"Can you show me the road they will take?" I ask as I consider my options.

"Sure!" Jerry replies excitedly, "Follow me."

We climb a steep path to the top of the mountain, where jagged peaks and deep crevices extend for as far as I can see. Jerry leads me along a rough trail which meanders through the strange landscape. Few plants grow on the plateau, and those that do are stumpy looking shrubs. The sun is high in the sky before we reach our destination.

Jerry stands on a slight rise and points downward as he says, "That path is the only way through the mountains."

I survey the area for a moment, and then ask, "That looks like an obvious place for a trap, why would they travel through there?"

Jerry nods excitedly as he replies, "We are at peace with our neighbors, and well inside the border. Besides, no one attacks the Royal Guard, not even the few bandit gangs that exist."

"Well," I reply, "I think we will do the obvious, and see what happens."

Jerry scratches his head and frowns, "The obvious?" he asks, clearly baffled.

I point at the trail, and then at the mountain peaks on either side as I explain, "We will create rockslides, cutting off the king from his guards. Your people will collapse this side, and I shall do the other."

"My people?" Jerry questions fearfully.

"Yes, your people!" I state, and then add, "If you want the crown, you are going to have to do some of the dirty work."

Jerry grumbles under his breath, "I suppose so."

"Good!" I reply, and then turn to leave.

Jerry stammers, "What are we to do?"

I turn to look at him and state, "We will prepare both sides of the pass, so that we are ready."

We spend the rest of the day on top of the mountain preparing two areas. My plan is to isolate the king from the bulk of his troops. Once we are done, Jerry staggers off, exhausted. I stare across at the other mountain top, evaluating where to set up similar rockslides. I decide to spend the next day working on the traps.

Madcat purrs loudly when I return, which makes me feel good. I eat heartily and sleep well. I arise early in the morning and travel alone to the mountain peak I had been scrutinizing yesterday.

It is well into the afternoon before I find locations suitable to prepare more rockslides. The sun is setting by the time I am finished. I gaze at my handiwork and nod appraisingly. Four separate areas are ready, two on each side that oppose one another. The results should be quite effective. I return to the villa, and then wait for word from Jerry.

A hammering on my door instantly wakes me. My scales harden instinctively as I demand hotly, "Who is this?"

"Jerry," he replies meekly, "the King is on the move." He hastily adds.

I arise, glance at the early rays of sunlight, and then walk to the door. Opening it reveals Jerry. He is obviously nervous and excited at the same time. He grins as he speaks, "I have eleven volunteers who will assist us. Will that be enough?" He asks gingerly.

"Plenty," I reply.

"Do you need some people on your side?" Jerry asks, though it is clear from his tone that he hopes I say no.

I stare intently at Jerry for a moment, making him squirm, and then allay his fears, "No, your people need to be on this mountain." I then issue my instructions, and have Jerry repeat them back to me, until I am certain he knows exactly what to do.

I gulp down a quick meal, and then hastily make my way to the mountain on the far side of the pass. I am concerned that the King's group will get there first, even though Jerry assures me it will take them until late afternoon to reach the area.

Arriving at the top of the mountain, I quickly scan my surroundings. As soon as I confirm that everything is in order, I look across to where Jerry's people are. I nod approvingly when I see two groups of people in the distance. I turn my attention to the path where King's troop is expected be traversing, and scowl as I crouch down. An advanced scout party of eight is slowly walking along the pass, and clearly scrutinizing the area. They look my way, but do not see me. The group walks the past, and then four of them return the way they came.

I stay out of sight as I move to a position ahead of the expected forces and wait. I can hear them before I see them. The sound of hundreds of powerful hoof beats strikes the ground, reverberating off the canyon walls. I lift my head and grin; the lead forces are turning into the canyon pathway. Metal glints and sparkles in the sunlight, it is almost the same armor I saw years ago, when I was impaled to a tree.

Jerry was right about the numbers, at least one hundred men ride beasts, while dozens of others run around on foot, tending to various needs, or scouting ahead. The entire force moves at a leisurely pace, one of indifference. The guards do not seem overly attentive, and their formation is not fixed. The King's carriage is at the mid-point, and is being pulled by six large beasts, the same kind the guards are riding.

The lead elements cross below me. I grab a piece of twine and pull hard. The other end of the twine is attached to a branch, one that is the thickness of my wrist. The branch slides back, releasing a large boulder, one of many which were painstakingly balanced upon one another.

The second my boulders begin to fall, I stand, and in full view of the guards below sprint along the mountain top to a similar pile of rocks near the rear of the mass of troops. On the other mountain side, Jerry's people unleash two more rockslides.

Dozens of massive boulders fall, causing chaos below as riders attempt to flee, and avoid being crushed.

I arrive at the last rock pile, and quickly release the boulders which tumble and fall down the steep mountain side. The men below are in disarray. The lead elements are cut off from the carriage, as are the rear. Smaller rockslides continue, sending dirt and debris down the sides of the mountains, adding to the chaos.

I review the disrupted forces and am pleased at the results of the rock falls. The King's carriage, along with around thirty guards, is trapped between two massive piles of rocks. I move out of sight, and then sprint down the path toward the rear elements of the soldiers, those separated from the carriage.

I come upon the forces and find them dismounted and clearing rocks. The first of them dies instantly as my claws penetrate his neck, severing his spinal column with a one quick slash. Two more fall prey to my razor-sharp claws, before the others realize I am in their midst. Six men rush at me with raised swords. I dive at their feet, slashing and gouging with my hands and feet as I roll between them. Without hesitation, I stand and charge three more. I drive my fist into the face of one man, shattering his nose in a fountain of blood. I then roll my claws into his eyes, driving them into his brain, then pull my hand away. He falls to the ground twitching, spasms racking his body.

A handful of men climb onto their mounts and flee, the rest turn to face me, weapons raised. I run at the remaining men, slashing, and gouging as I get to them. Their weapons deflect off my scales and do little damage. A man stabs at me with a spear. I twist and turn and feel the spear tip scrape along my side. I grab the spear with both hands and spin around, ripping it from the soldier's hands. He screams as I thrust at him. His scream is cut off as I drive the point into his throat.

There are seven men standing between me and the rocks, all that remains of the group. Behind them is the massive pile of rocks, beyond which is my target, the King. One of the men licks his lips in fear, the others hold their weapons nervously. They move skittishly on their feet then, as one, they drop their weapons and run. I pay them little heed and climb the rocks. Arriving at the top I see the King's carriage before me, surrounded by some forty men.

I stand tall and roar loudly while beating my chest. My scales harden more, becoming heavy plates. I leap from rock to rock as I descend into the pit with the men who are defending their King. Ten of them charge at me, screaming and waving their swords as if to intimidate me. I slow down and wait for them to get closer. I drop to the ground and spin around, knocking three of them down with my legs. Two of the men will never rise, the contents of their stomachs spilling onto the ground. The remaining man rolls over and holds his ruined intestines with his hands.

I roll once more, narrowly avoiding a massive sword which clangs on the ground where my head rested a split second ago. Jumping to my feet I grab the nearest man, and spin him around, lifting him off the ground completely. I spin faster and faster, striking two more down with the screaming man. I shove as I let him go, causing him to fly head-first into the rock wall where his scream is cut short by a thud. He slides to the ground, leaving a trail of brains in his wake. I immediately jump onto the two men that were knocked down and drive my rearward claws deeply into their bodies. I twist my feet as I turn and leap away, slicing them widely open. The men cough blood as they attempt to hold their ruined bodies together.

An arrow strikes my back, and ricochets harmlessly away. Another narrowly misses my head, causing me to dodge and weave my way through a growing number of projectiles. Rolling toward the nearest man, I drive my open claws through his weak armor, and into his chest. Standing, I use his body as a shield as I close the distance to the archers. The man moans as arrows impale his body. Unbelievably, he is still clinging to life when I hurl him at a group of three men. The impact causes all four men to fall to the ground, entangled in each other. I use the discord to strike at another man, cleaving his head completely from his body. A massive fountain of blood shoots out as he falls to the ground, spraying those around him.

For fifteen minutes I hack, slash, and cleave bodies into bloody pulp. Striding to the carriage I shatter the door, revealing a man cowering in fear. My black scales being covered in the blood and entrails of his guards, adds to his terror.

He raises his hands and says, "Whatever you are, I hope you understand me. I will pay any ransom; do anything you want."

I advance menacingly to him as I reply, "Yes, you will die!"

He holds his hands up to ward me off. I strike swiftly, shattering the bones in his arms with one sweep of my arm. I drive a claw into his chest, and slash downward, spilling his entrails onto his legs.

I leave the carriage, and then make my way to the last group of men, on the far side of the second rock fall. As before, I stand at the top of the rock pile and roar to the guards. But instead of attacking them, I turn and flee. Glancing back, I am pleased to see them pursuing me. I maintain a steady pace as I escape, allowing them to keep me in their sights.

I lope toward the plain, and away from Jerry's villa. My pursuers make good time and begin to catch up. I feel a surge of adrenaline when I see a handful of men riding animals. I pick up my pace, but not so much that they will lose interest. Every now and then I slow, to let them catch up. I frown with concern when I see the men who are on foot returning to the mountain pass.

I continue onward, luring and drawing my pursuers toward the distant lava flows. The chase begins to tire me, reminding me that my endurance does have limits. As the men close the distance, I begin to doubt my ability to stay ahead of them. Glancing left and right, I notice a thicket of woods not too far away. I dash toward them and blindly charge into the trees. The thunder of approaching hooves boosts my adrenaline. Branches scratch at my scales as I run through the undergrowth.

Panting heavily, I stop and look back to where I entered. Branches sway back and forth from my passage, but there is no sign of my pursuers. I tilt my head and listen intently, then I hear it, a voice issuing instructions. I grin as I prepare for the armed men.

The first man to enter the thicket has no chance. I strike his head so hard it flies in the air and rolls out toward the other men. The man's body falls to the ground, his life's blood spurting over the foliage. Two more men charge in, swords raised and at the ready, but I have gone. I quietly move away from the trap and wait as groups of men swing in from either side. Their plan to draw me into a fight at the edge of the woods, has failed.

I come up behind four men and attack. I slash one down his back so deeply his spine pops out from his body. Another turns at the sounds of his dying comrade. I rake his face with my claws, tearing out an eyeball with my downward slash. His screams draw the attention of another group, which turns my way. The remaining two men yell as they charge at me with their swords raised. I dodge and deflect their blows, then spin around. My rearward claw slashes the first man across his stomach, spilling his innards onto the ground. Unexpectedly my claw lodges into the second man's rib cage. We both stare, perplexed at the sight for a moment, then blood begins to pour from my victim's mouth. I yank my foot clear, tearing a pair of ribs from his chest in the process. He coughs up a huge gout of blood as he clutches his ruined chest, then falls face first to the ground.

The approaching group slows, they number seven men, and clearly their resolve is wavering. I jump toward them and howl loudly. As one, they drop their weapons and flee in terror. One of the men is so scared he runs into an old tree branch, impaling himself on it. He groans and writhes as he tries to pull himself free. I stride up to the struggling man, and slide him off the branch, leaving it slick with his blood. I pick him up and with all my might hurl him through the forest's edge. He falls to the ground with a painful grunt and rolls to a stop at the foot of a man who is still atop his beast. The injured man's glazed eyes stare upward as his life seeps away.

I collect the discarded weapons, and then wait for the next assault.

I smell it before I see it, a faint burning smell. They have set the woods on fire! I do not hesitate, I drop the weapons, and flee.

I exit the woods, away from the beast riders, and sprint as fast as I can. The men pursue, and to my surprise their numbers have grown. Fortunately, stopping in the woods has rejuvenated my energy, providing me with renewed stamina. I draw on my fresh vitality and push myself to surge farther ahead of the riders.

The stream we crossed during the trek to Jerry's is up ahead; it is the same stream which runs near my cave. The sound of hoof beats gets louder as the beast riders get closer. I run parallel to the creek for a while and then finding the widest deepest section, leap across with all my might. I land on the far bank then turn around and grin. Some of the riders pull their beasts to a stop, while others plunge into the deeper waters.

One of the men hurls a spear at me. I easily dodge the weapon, and then retrieve it. The man stares across the water in fear as I lift the spear up and point it at him. He turns and runs. I feel the weight and balance of the weapon and then heave it at the fleeing figure. The spear flies fast and true, and lodges in the man's lower back. The impact is so great; he is knocked down. The tip of the spear exits his stomach and digs into the dirt, holding his body up for a moment. His screams echo around the landscape as his arms and legs flail while he slides down the shaft to the ground.

Another man stares at his own spear, and then turns and looks at me fearfully. A few of his colleagues are making their way up and down stream, seeking easier ways across. I take advantage of their disarray, and lope away at a steady pace.

To my surprise, the men give up the chase. I watch from a distance as they head back. I recall Jerry's words about the patrols and continue to the lava flows. Arriving, I set up a massive fire pit. I hunt down and kill a grazing beast, cook it, and then feast on the meat. I make sure to leave as many tracks as I can in the area, and even traipse up and down the nearby hills a few times. I stay in the hill region for two days, leaving the bones of my kills scattered, as an animal would.

On the third day, my patience is rewarded. A rising dust cloud, and the thunder of hundreds of hoof beats, heralds the approach of the force I have been expecting. I stare into the distance and count at least three hundred riders, quite a formidable number. I stand up on the hill, in plain sight, and roar loudly at the approaching army. I watch as they break off into three groups. One group rides straight at me, while the others are clearly planning on flanking my position.

I raise my arms high in the air and roar once more, then I turn and flee. I run down the incline, and then straight up the next hill, ignoring the path that runs to either side. I jump from boulder to boulder and keep well away from the soft soil. The slope is steep, so I drop to all fours to make my climb easier. I arrive at the top just as the first of the riders appear on both paths. I crouch down behind a stack of boulders and wait.

The three groups converge on the campsite that I had set up, and then they fan out, searching. They point excitedly at my prints, and follow them, while others gaze around with a mixture of fear and excitement. A few glance my way, but when they cannot find any tracks, dismiss the slope. I sit back and relax as I watch the soldiers search for me. Eventually the men make camp, and then settle in for the night.

I study the patrol routes they are establishing and am impressed. My plan will be difficult to implement. I stare up at the star filled sky, and grin at the clouds that are rolling in. My plan just got easier.

I wait for half the night to pass, and as the clouds cover the stars slowly make my way down the slope, heading for the extreme edge of their camp. Once there, I crouch down behind a large bounder, and wait.

I do not have to wait long. The three men in the patrol are chatting and paying little attention to their surroundings as they walk along the path. I pick up a fist sized rock, and as they get close, hurl it over their heads. It strikes the far side of the hill with a thud and causes a small amount of dirt to slide. The men spin around and lift their weapons. I leap over the bolder and land on two of them. They scream as my weight drives them to the ground. Slashing at the third with my claws, I catch him in the neck, severing a main artery. He falls to the ground, gurgling and drowning on his blood. The two men beneath me thrash and squirm as I dig my heels into them, driving my main claws into their bodies. I leap away, tearing flesh as I do.

I can hear more men shouting and hurrying toward me. I turn and run down the path, away from the camp, leaving bloody prints as I go. The men find their torn apart comrades and stop. I turn back and with my night vision watch as they rally their forces.

I pause, perplexed, I had expected a group to chase me, instead they are bolstering the patrols, and waiting. It would seem they are learning. I stand and listen intently, then begin to make my way around to the far side of their camp.

Walking stealthily, I notice a solitary guard standing near a pile of rocks. I am perplexed, until the smell of his urine wafts my way. I rush at him, he turns at the sound of my approach, but he is too slow. I slice his throat open before he can make any noise, and then sever his arms and legs. I toss them aside, to make it appear as if he were pulled apart by some great force.

I spend the night dispatching a dozen others, and then as the early morning rays of sunrise appear, I leave the area. I make my way slowly and cautiously to Jerry's villa. I imagine the panic on the soldier's faces when they find their torn apart comrades.

As I make my way across the plain my stomach growls, reminding me that I have not eaten for a while. I scan the horizon, looking for signs of soldiers, and seeing none, I begin my hunt for one of the many grazing beasts that live in the region. Taking one down is easy; eating the raw flesh and drinking its blood satisfies me. I stare at the carcass and leave it. There are many other predators in the area, and they should make short work of what is left.

I glance at the darkening skies, and the angry clouds which are fast approaching. Wind gusts nip at my heels as I hurry toward the villa. Approaching the hillside pathway, I notice movement and immediately stop. Droplets of rain land on me, forming rivulets of water which run down my scales. I crouch down in the long grass and wait.

The minutes pass, but eventually my patience is rewarded when I hear a brief cough. I search the rocks intently, and then spot the man. A guard dressed as those from the castle. His mouth is moving. He is talking to someone, someone out of sight. I slowly shift my position, and then spot the person he is talking to. The pair of soldiers appear to be guarding the way to Jerry's villa.

As I cautiously make my way to the hillside, I wonder what their purpose is. Are they holding Jerry under house arrest? Or has Jerry double crossed me? The rainfall increases in intensity as thunder and lightning fill the sky. I travel away from the path, to the side of the hill, where I stare at the water cascading down the steep slope. My powerful claws easily propel me up the slippery incline. Avoiding another pair of soldiers is relatively easy. I debate over how to enter the villa. I grin as the solution becomes abundantly clear. Leaping as hard as I can, I catch the balcony railing, and clamber over it just as another pair of soldiers appear on the street.

I am greeted by growls as I step into the bed chamber. Madcat crouches on the floor, her ears flat against her head. As soon as she recognizes me, she quits growling, and pads over to me. Scrutinizing the room reveals that it is as I left it. I listen at the door to the main house, and then upon hearing nothing, cautiously open it. Now, I can hear a heated discussion coming from downstairs.

"I told you," Jerry states, "Not only did we have nothing to do with the attack, I am the rightful heir, and when the time is right, I shall present myself at the castle."

"You are nothing but a peasant!" Replies a gruff voice.

"I will present myself, and my proof, at the castle in a few days," Jerry responds authoritatively. He then demands, "Your soldiers should leave!"

The gruff voice responds sardonically, "They are here for your protection, Sire!"

I retire to my room and close the door as quietly as I can. I search my pouches and find the ring Jerry handed to me. What an archaic society, that such a thing is proof of a man's linage. I stare at the signet ring, and then notice a small oddity in the engraving, an unusual shape. I ponder its significance, and then decide to ask Jerry when I am able.

I lay on the bed and listen to the sounds from the outside. The footfalls of the villa's inhabitants are softer than the soldiers, whose hard boots and stern gait easily identify their passage. The soldiers are cussing and swearing at their duty, with some blaming Jerry's people for the king's death. Others express their doubts. I begin to smile as I hear one soldier recount how he barely survived my attack. He talks of being quick enough to have avoided my death swipe.

I awake with a start; someone is entering my room. Madcat growls menacingly and prowls near the door. I roll out of bed and move to a position behind the opening door. A large dish slides into the room, then the door is quickly slammed shut. I stare at the dish and quietly chuckle, the kitchen staff is feeding Madcat. I glance around the room and wonder who lets her out, as there is no mess anywhere. I glance to the balcony, and then grin widely; it seems that I am not the only one to think of jumping up here. I secure the door, and then rest once more.

The morning sunlight strikes the balcony as I awake. I rise and open the door then, upon hearing nothing, make my way downstairs. A young boy comes running across the room, and as soon as he sees me, he back pedals, falls, and then slides to a stop at my feet. The boy's eyes are wide with fear, but he does not scream. Perhaps he is too frightened to make a noise.

I smile at the boy and ask, "Where is Jerry?"

The boy stammers as he stands and backs away, "He is… he is… he is in the basement." The boy flees as fast as his feet can carry him.

I make my way to the basement, and am surprised at how spacious, clean, and well organized it is. The area is made up of a dozen large rooms, all radiating from a large central area which houses a large desk. Jerry is leaning on the desk and staring at some papers.

Jerry glances up and smiles. He motions for me to come closer as he says, "You did great! I am glad you made it back, safely."

"I lured them to the lava, as planned." I reply, then add, "I did not expect to see guards here when I returned!"

Jerry nods as he responds, "The guards are convinced that we caused the rockslides."

I stare at Jerry and then hand him his ring as I ask, "What does the shape of the engraving represent?"

Jerry grins, "My family has an unusual birthmark on our chests. It has been with us for four generations, and my son carries it, as well."

I recall the boy who was running around the villa and grin. I stare at Jerry and bluntly state, "I will continue to protect your family, as agreed."

Jerry nods excitedly as he takes the offered ring and stares at it, "This villa will become your private home. I will make sure that only the most trusted people live and work here, to maintain it."

I sense Jerry's sincerity as I stare intently at him. His eyes do not waver from mine as he holds out his arm. I take his in mine, carefully keeping my claws retracted, and grip him firmly. We release after a few seconds, with no words being spoken or needed.

Long Live the King

Jerry departs with most of the villa's inhabitants, along with all the soldiers. I immediately begin crafting and installing small solar panels on the villa's roof tiles. These panels are black and absorb virtually all light. My crafting tool is drained each evening, but thanks to the additional panels, it charges quickly each morning.

It is three days before a messenger arrives, one who carries wonderful news. Jerry's right to the crown has been established beyond any measure of doubt. One of his first decrees was to order patrols to keep a look out for a strange beast, which was last seen near the lava fields. I grin at that piece of news as it should keep the soldiers well away from this area. He has also decreed that his villa be held in trust for his son, and thus is off limits to all but his own personal guard, many of whom are inhabitants that know of my existence, and the help I gave Jerry.

The days pass quickly, and as I add more panels to the roof, I realize that I will need a power cell from the shuttle in order to capitalize on the energy potential. I stare at the darkening skies and decide that a night-time trek would be best. I make sure no one sees me leave and make quick time across the plain. I hear the bubbling creek before I see it and cross it easily. I arrive near my cave just as the morning sun begins to peek across the valley.

The rocks which we piled in front of the entrance remain exactly as Jerry and I left them. I remove just enough to allow me to crawl into the main cave. I climb the secondary wall inside, and find the shuttle is also exactly as I left it. I disconnect its secondary power cell, and then remove the cylinder and rest it on the pilot's chair. It is not heavy, but its smooth edges will make it difficult to carry.

I stand and ponder what to do. My eyes suddenly focus on the solution, one that is right in front of me, an old animal skin. Within ten minutes I have fashioned a crude backpack, and after testing its strength, I place the power cell in it, and then leave. The space I crawled through is too small to wear the pack, so I push it ahead of me as I crawl out.

Sealing the cave once more takes little time; there is still ample daylight left, so I put the backpack on and begin the journey back to the villa. The sun is setting as I approach the vast plain, but I forge on. Under the cover of darkness, I reenter the villa, and then quietly return to my room. Madcat pads over to me and rubs her head on my thighs, purring loudly as she does.

I lay on the bed and relax. I open my eyes to find that I have slept well past sunrise. I get up and stretch, then make my way to the kitchen where I startle a pair of cooks.

I grin as I tell them, "I am just looking for something to eat."

One of the cooks, a nervous young girl, prepares a large plate full of meat, and hands it to me with shaky hands.

"Thank you," I respond as I take the offered food.

She scurries away without uttering a word, she is clearly terrified.

"I would never harm a friend!" I inform them matter-of-factly.

I take the plate to my room and share the meat with Madcat. Once sated, I continue my project. I climb up into the rafters and position the power cell so that it is hidden from below. It takes time to manufacture the wiring required, but time is something I have.

The days turn into weeks as I painstakingly turn the entire roof into a massive solar collector. Once done I monitor the power flow, and then calculate how long the cell will take to charge. I blink in disdain at the numbers and run them again.

I sit back, close my eyes, and mumble to myself, "Two hundred fifty-seven cycles."

I stare up at the ceiling and wonder what else I can do. As I sit there, the answer becomes clear, and although it will take time, I realize I will have to add solar panels to every rooftop.

The weeks fly by as I work on the rooftops of each of the buildings. Finally, as the days shorten and the nights become colder, my task is done. The few people who maintain the buildings become less fearful of me, as they finally realize that my word is my bond. Some of them actually strike up brief conversations, which I find pleases me.

The young girl who works in the kitchen approaches me and with her eyes lowered and asks, "Aren't you afraid of the snow?"

I frown at her unusual question and respond, "No, why?"

"We have little wood, and these houses get cold." She replies meekly.

I stand quickly, which causes the girl to step back fearfully. I shake my head as I inform her, "Do not be afraid, I think I can help."

I mentally chastise myself. I have been on every rooftop, and these buildings have no insulation against the cold. Retiring to my room, I take out my crafting tool and ponder what it can make. Within a short amount of time I come upon a solution. The same insulation that is used in the Protectorate's spacecraft, bioduropoly, should serve these buildings well.

The material is an exceedingly thin complex polymer and takes considerable energy and time to fabricate. I decide to directly bond the material to the outside of the buildings, starting at the ground and working my way up. The days pass quickly as I work methodically. Blocking the drafts alone in these archaic buildings would make a difference, even without the thermal properties of the material I am applying.

The curious townsfolk begin to watch what I am doing, but it is clear from their murmurings and mumblings they do not believe that what I am doing will help. I am still working on the upper walls of my villa when the first snow falls. I decide to leave the roofs alone; the vast number of solar panels has already made a considerable difference in the amount of heat that escapes. With the buildings being heated by open fireplaces, I leave the air space in the joints between the roof and the walls, for the smoke to escape.

A pair of guards walk by, stamping their feet to keep warm. I frown as I turn to them and ask, "Where were you, to get so cold?"

The pair point at the trail as one of them says, "We have a shelter we use. We are instructed to guard the trail at all times."

"Show me," I demand.

The men reluctantly turn and lead me to their shelter. I stare at it in disbelief, it is no more than a few planks thrown over a couple of large boulders.

The back of the shelter is the cliff face the trail follows.

I turn to the men and state, "I will make this fit for your duty."

The men blink and stare in disbelief as I tear their shelter down and begin to move rocks and build a more solid wall. I turn to them and say, "Go and warm yourselves. This will take some time."

The men happily leave the biting cold and trudge their way up the trail.

Turning back to my task, I replace the planks, and use them as guides for a layer of bioduropoly. I add a lining of this material to both sides of the planks. Using more rocks and small boulders, I design a small path, and create an antechamber to the guard post.

I spend three days on the shelter, sending the guards back each time they check on my progress. I add solar panels to the roof, and then manufacture heating elements along the lower walls. These heaters cast a soft glow and will serve as indirect lighting as well as being able to heat the enclosed space. I craft a battery, which I install in a small recess in the wall. Next, I add seven, small, clear windows for the guards to see out of, and add slits, which can be sealed off, for archers to fire their arrows through. Adding doors to either side of the antechamber will minimize the heat loss as the guards come and go.

Once done, I stand back, and grin with pride at my construct. From a distance, it looks like the cliff wall into which it is built, and even when approaching, it does not appear to be a guard post until the windows are noticed. As I stare, it suddenly dawns on me, I crafted a battery. I should be able to turn the entire basement of my villa into a series of batteries, and then all I have to do is bring the shuttle here and charge its primary cell.

The guards, all twenty of them, give me their seal of approval on the guard post. For them, what used to be a dreary and cold duty, is not only more pleasant, they finally see me as a friend, and not a monster.

As soon as I return to the villa, I begin work on the basement. The young girl who works in the kitchen, spends a lot of time watching me. I am not sure if this is out of fear, or fascination. I turn to her and ask, "Your name is Natalie, correct?"

"Yes." She replies meekly.

"I am Mamluk!" I proudly respond.

Natalie frowns as if confused, and then asks, "How can you speak when your mouth is so large and full of long sharp teeth?"

I chuckle as I reply, "I could ask you the same thing. Your mouths are so small, and yet you are able to make a lot of noise."

"I have never seen any more of your kind. Where are you from?" Natalie asks inquisitively.

I consider how to tell this illiterate waif where I am from. "Follow me," I state as I step outside.

Natalie grabs a shawl as she trails behind, her curiosity getting the better of her now. The snow is falling in great quantities today. The light breeze piles deep drifts of it up against the sides of the buildings. She shudders as she steps outside and says, "It's cold out here."

I grin as I reply, "The insulation is working well." I then point up to the skies and, even though they are filled with clouds, envisage the millions of stars that exist beyond them. "I come from one of the lights in the sky."

She stares at me in awe, her mouth wide open. A moment later she either stammers or shivers, as she asks, "But why did you come here?"

"Everyone is somewhere, and I am here," I reply cryptically.

She scrunches her nose up at my answer, clearly not impressed, and says, "I have to go inside, it's too cold for me."

I watch as she steps back into the villa, and then after gazing around the landscape for a moment, follow her and shut the door.

"Hey," I call out after her, "Would you like to pet Madcat?"

Natalie spins around excitedly and says, "Would she let me?"

Without a second of hesitation she runs up the stairs and waits outside my chamber. I open the door and walk to the sleeping animal. I stroke her fur, as I instruct, "You can approach her. She won't hurt you. You have my word."

Natalie gingerly stretches her hand out and strokes Madcat's tan fur. The animal purrs. Natalie jumps back fearfully, and stares at the animal with wide eyes.

I feel a strange sense of contentment as I inform the girl, "That sound simply means that Madcat was enjoying your touch."

She steps closer and pets Madcat once more. It does not take her long before her confidence has her stroking Madcat's head, neck, and back. She even rubs her face into Madcat's neck, which makes me smile.

Madcat opens her eyes and stares at Natalie for a moment, and then rolls on her side. Natalie warily rubs her belly. Suddenly she notices the scar on her chest and gasps, "What happened to her?"

"A soldier stabbed her with a spear, a long time ago."

Natalie is genuinely concerned as she gently rubs Madcat's fur. She looks at me with an odd expression and says, "Is that why you helped Jerry become the King, so the soldiers wouldn't hurt these animals anymore?"

I tilt my head at the revelation that his uneducated girl came up with an idea, which I had never thought of, and yet I should have. "That is a great idea," I reply. Nodding in agreement, I add, "We should make sure that these creatures are protected."

The front door to the villa blows violently open, and slams against the wall. Its hinges squeal in protest as the thump of its impact reverberates around the villa.

I point to Natalie and warn her, "Stay here."

I rush to the steps, and down to the main level. Strong winds are blowing through the door, covering a blood trail. I force the doors shut, securely bolt them, then follow the blood.

Three people are tending to a soldier, one of the trusted guards assigned to protect this villa. A long arrow protrudes from his chest, his facial hair is matted with blood, more froths from his mouth and nose with every breath.

He weakly points to me and mumbles, "Bandits."

I move the others out of the way, and quickly tend to the man's wound. The arrow is deep. The man groans in pain as I grab it and pull. The arrow comes out with a long sucking sound, followed by the man's scream as he loses consciousness. Thankfully the arrow tip is small, and not barbed. The medical supplies in my pouches are sufficient to cauterize the wound and close the hole. I am cautious in their use, but once done, I notice that I am down to less than half of what I started with.

These are precious minutes that I could have been outside dealing with the bandits, but the man had little time if he were to be saved. He stood guard, to protect this villa, and that loyalty deserves reward.

As soon as I am finished, I issue my instructions, "Lock the door behind me. No one is to go outside. Understood?"

The three people nod fearfully, then follow me to the door. I open it and make my way into the howling snows as they close it behind me. I search the area intently but can find no sign of anyone. I cautiously make my way down the trail to the guard post where I see a body partially laying in a snow drift. Numerous arrows are sticking out from it. It appears as though the bandits waited for the changing of the guard to attack.

Once again, I search the area, and then I notice a heat source. A group of seven are resting on the leeward side of the hill. Their vantage point allows them to see the rear door to the guard post, and the path I am standing on. I slowly back up, and then make my way to a position above them. I then wait, and watch. The time passes slowly while the bandits simply sit. The snow falls steadily as the wind ebbs and flows, creating drifts across the path.

The door to the guard post opens, and as one the seven figures stand and begin to raise their bows. I drop down in their midst, and land squarely on one of them. I hack and slash at the bandits with my claws. Their thick layers of furs protect them a little, but not enough. Within seconds the man I landed on is dead, as are four others. Two more lay on the ground, covered in their own blood, and holding themselves. One has a massive gash across his chest, from which blood freely flows. Another is trying hold his intestines in, but the rope-like innards slowly spill out regardless.

I grab the bandit's guts, and as I pull them from his body demand, "How many more of you? Answer, and I shall end your misery quickly."

He moans, shakes his head, then convulses and dies. I turn to the other survivor and repeat my demand.

The bandit spits a bloody gout of phlegm at me, and shouts, "Go to hell you monster!" The exertion causes a fresh surge of blood to cover his hands.

I stomp savagely on the man's chest with my foot, crushing his rib cage, killing him instantly. I lift my gaze and, through the falling snow, search the area intently. I can find no more signs of bandits.

I stride to the guard post and shout, "I am Mamluk! It is safe now."

Two men exit the building, they nervously glance left and right as if they are about to be attacked. I maintain a watchful eye as I question the guards, "Did you see any more attackers?"

One of the men shakes his head as he replies, "The first we knew of them was when they shot arrows at our replacements."

I frown as I notice a heat signature in the distance. I turn to the guards and instruct them, "Go to the Villa, wake everyone, and prepare for an attack."

The men glance around anxiously, nod, and then fearfully scurry off. I focus on the distant heat source and wonder what it could be. The indiscernible mass is approaching the base of the path that leads to the villa. Staring intently, I notice two small dots approaching the mass.

"Scouts!" I shout into the snow filled wind.

I shake my head in aggravation over what looks to be a large force coming this way. I return to the villa and am pleased to see sentries on the lookout. Once inside, I gather all but the sentries in the large main hall. The locals are all quite familiar with my appearance, and none seem bothered, or afraid of me, as they first were.

I cast my gaze over the people, and in a loud voice state, "There is a large force approaching this community, and based on the earlier attack, they would appear to be hostile."

Many of the group shift their feet nervously, while others glance around with mounting apprehension.

I hold up my hand to quiet the murmurs and continue, "We will prepare a trap for them, one they will never expect. Do as I say, and you will all survive this."

Before anyone can lose focus, I begin issuing instructions. Soon, I have teams of people outside, preparing what I hope is a deadly surprise for the approaching force. Once I see that everyone is galvanized into action, I walk outside to join those already working, and smile at the progress they are making.

The teams are busily digging four long furrows in the snow, down the sloping path. Using my craft tool, I line the furrows with a thick layer of white powder. It is an inorganic compound, one which I expect will terrify the incoming force. The compound blends in well with the snow and is soon covered by fresh flakes. I then fashion a simple fuse wire, which I run off to one side.

A group hurries to the bodies of the slain. The deceased guard is left exactly as he is, but they remove all signs of those I killed, along with my tracks. As a final touch they leave the outer door to the guard post open, allowing it to fill with snow. They take one of the bandit's bodies and dress it in the leather armor from the wounded man. They place this body face down, a short distance from the first body, and closer to the villa.

As soon as the furrows are about fifty paces long, I send everyone inside to warm up. I have barely finished when I notice a small group of fur-covered individuals approaching. They are too far away to see me, but I take no chances, and retreat to the Villa.

The second I step inside, I state, "The first of the scouts are approaching. Leave them be and let them report back to their main force. Once they are gone, I want you all to assume your positions."

One group makes their way upstairs and waits out of sight with their arrows at the ready. The rest prepare their weapons, and then also quietly wait.

I stride outside but keep my distance from the approaching figures. I watch as five of them cautiously pass the slain guard, and then the second body, which they seem to assume is the other guard. They examine the area and then make their way to where I had killed their colleagues. Once there, they debate in hushed tones about what transpired. Finally, being unable to explain what happened to the bodies, I can hear one of them mention desertion. The group then slinks way, disappearing into the increasing snowfall.

I rush back to the villa and give my signal. The men upstairs step out onto the balcony, crouch down and wait. Others hurry from the villa and conceal themselves in vantage points on either side of the path. The heavy snow soon covers their tracks and cloaks, making them virtually undetectable. I walk to the end of the fuse wire, crouch, and wait.

Minutes later the first of the group of trespassers come into sight, soon followed by dozens more. The groups fade in and out of view through the blowing snow. A large group walks slowly past the far end of the concealed furrows; another follows close behind. As soon as the first group approaches the top of the furrows, I light the fuse wire. It weakly splutters and sparkles as it trails toward the top of the furrows.

The second the lit wire reaches the furrows; the heat causes an amazing chemical reaction. Massive tendrils of material begin to rise into the air. Spikes and spires seem to grow from the ground, then gravity pulls them over, where more are already forming. The reaction is so fast and powerful, that within seconds the top of the furrows become one mass, which dwarfs the tallest of the invaders.

The approaching force retreats fearfully as the chain reaction works its way down the furrows, seemingly chasing them. I grin as I see the second part of my plan coming into play.

Natalie, who is dressed in bright clothing, walks to the top of the hill, then looks down at the bandits and hollers, "I conjure my defender!" She quickly scurries out of sight, to avoid being struck by any arrows.

The bandits are too awe struck to bother attacking her, which is fortunate, as she has put herself in danger. I stealthily make my way to a position in the midst of the mass which blocks the path. The chemical reaction has run its course, leaving a tangled mass which looks impressive, but in reality, is quite fragile.

I roar loudly, my noise echoing around the hills, and then thrash at the mass, shattering material in all directions. I then run through the mass toward the bandits. I imagine that all they can see at this stage is something coming through the wall of strange substance which rose from the ground.

I burst out from the end and charge the first man. I slash at his face, slicing to the bone. The second man fares no better, as my left hand crushes his skull. A third falls backward as he attempts to retreat. I leap onto his body and dig my clawed heels into his chest, puncturing his lungs. His last breath escapes him as a bloody wheeze.

An arrow flies past my shoulder, missing me by a good margin. I dive at the next handful of men, clawing and slashing as I plow through them. I glance up and see the final phase of my plan coming into play. Dozens of arrows streak over my head from the villa. I don't expect any to hit anyone, but they do add to the effect I wanted to create. The bandits turn and run.

Before any of the attackers can rally themselves, I vanish into the howling snows, retreating toward the villa. I work my way around to the side of the hill, and then cautiously make my way back toward the bandits.

A handful of them are attempting to rally the others, but with little success. I catch a few words and frown, "Boy… easy… not dying for…" The howling winds prevent me from catching anything else.

The bandits regroup, and then leave. I ponder their words, and then decide to follow them. I stay well behind the group. Through the falling snow I can see that they number around thirty individuals. Once well out into the plain, the group stops and sets up a crude camp. They form a retaining wall out of snow, which deflects much of the wind, and then build a small fire. I watch, as each member contributes a piece of wood to the fire.

I consider attacking them but decide that the risk is too great. I would have to face all of them at once, and being cornered, they would probably fight with greater determination. The driving wind and bitter cold has little effect on my scales, but even so, sitting and waiting is beginning to take its toll. Reluctantly I return to the villa.

Chapter Three – Everything Changes

The seasons come and go as I work to utilize the primitive technology available to charge the power cell. The cellar is lined with wood burning boilers which provide a trickle of electricity, while every rooftop in the villa is covered with solar panels. But even with all these measures, I will still be marooned on this planet for a considerable time.

Madcat is showing her age, and pads around the villa with a pronounced limp. No one is afraid of her anymore; instead she enjoys the many friendly pats and belly rubs she receives. The young kitchen girl, Natalie, is now a woman, one who runs the kitchen with a forceful will. She is married to one of the guards, and now has her own baby daughter, one who loves to hang onto Madcat's fur and get dragged along.

Jerry visits rarely these days, his duties as King keep him busy. I do not mind this, as the fewer people who know about this place, the better. The bandits never returned, and apart from an occasional traveler, the guards have little to do. I notice that they no longer take their duties as seriously as they once did, but then why would they? The bandit attack was many years ago.

I am sitting in the main hall when I hear a loud shout from outside. I hear a commotion; the sounds of steel clashing. Madcat lifts her head and growls menacingly. I motion for her to go upstairs, and then stride purposefully toward the main door.

The door bursts open before I can get to it. Three guards spill inside, all grievously wounded. Behind them is the King's Royal Guard, being led by an unfamiliar figure. I step out the door, and into the trap they set. Dozens of massive spears come at me. The spears carry a huge lattice of rope which rushes blazingly fast at me. I have little time to react but manage to leap backward into the villa. The spears impale the door frame, the rope lattice lurches inside for a moment, but is arrested by the spears.

I slam the door shut and side the bolt to lock secure it. I turn to see Natalie cradling one of the guards, her husband. He is dead, and the other two are not far from death themselves. The King's Royal Guard is attacking the villa's guards, slaughtering everyone. I consider the ramifications of the attack and cannot believe that Jerry would be behind this action, especially after all this time.

I turn to the handful of people who are fearfully looking at me and instruct them, "Gather everyone, and go to the cellar. There is a passageway that will lead us out."

Madcat limps to the stairs, crouches at my feet, and growls menacingly. I pat her and say, "Your days of fighting are long over old friend."

My face twitches as I realize that I will not have time to disconnect the power unit. I put it from my mind and lead Madcat down the steps. As I shut the door to the basement, I hear the villa's front door splintering. The sounds of axes hacking at the door herald its impending failure.

Long ago, I lined the basement door with bioduropoly in case of an explosion. The thin layer of armor is stronger than its depth implies and is quite resilient. I slide three massive wooden beams across the closed door, and then secure them firmly in place. The door will slow them down considerably, though I have no doubt that a determined force could still break through.

I notice that many of the group are looking around in fear. A couple of them begin rushing around in a panic, looking for a way out. I count at least twenty-three in all, including Natalie.

I stand tall and state, "The exit you seek is concealed. Come this way."

I lead the group to a stone wall, where I touch a small rock. The rock covers a switch; the wall is actually a stone covered electric door. The stone block slides smoothly back, and then pivots to one side, revealing a well-lit passageway. It slopes downward at a minor angle and extends as far as I can see.

I motion to the passage as I state, "I will set this basement to explode once they have breached the door. That should buy us time."

The group is apprehensive but does as instructed. They glance nervously at the lights as they hesitantly walk down the passage. Madcat picks up the rear, her limp slows her down considerably. I stare at the group, and in particular at my trusted companion, and wonder what will become of them all.

I turn to the main boiler, and sigh. So many years of effort, and now it has come to this. I crank the boiler up and close the safety release valves. The door has a small sensor which sends an alert when it is opened. I run the sensor to the side of the boiler and connect it to a small package. The explosive is more potent than anything this planet is able to manufacture, and should obliterate the room, if not the villa itself. I glance upward as I consider the power cell, and its chances of remaining functional.

With nothing left for me to do, I retreat into the passageway, and shut the stone wall, sealing it. Next, I disconnect the door's electric motor, and then drop wedges into three holes in the floor behind the stone. These should make the stone panel virtually immovable. As I finish, I hear the faint, yet distinct, sounds of axes chopping at the basement door.

I sprint away from the stone and catch up to the others relatively quickly. Seconds later a muffled boom resonates from behind. Dirt and sand falls from the ceiling, then the lights go out, plunging the passageway into darkness. Those around me gasp and utter expletives, but no one panics. Every third light flickers, then comes on, creating a pale dust filled glow. The small batteries in them will only last a short time, but it should be enough.

I slowly make my way through the group, reassuring them as I go. I get to the front, and then lead them down the long passageway. Finally, I come to a grey door, one covered with bioduropoly. I glance through the door's peephole and study the poorly lit cavern on the other side. Once I am satisfied that the cavern is empty, I open the door and step through. I wave for the others to follow me.

Once everyone is in the cavern, I close the door. Its rock covered exterior blends so well with the cave's wall, it is virtually impossible to see. If it were not for my enhanced vision, even I would not be able to detect it.

A few of those with me warily gaze outside. Their apprehension is a palpable presence, as is their fear. I go to the cave's opening and intently search the area. The cave is well away from the pathway leading to the villa, while the rocky outcroppings above hide the entrance. Stepping out and glancing upward reveals tendrils of smoke rising from where the villa would be.

I sigh, and then motion to those inside the cave as I quietly instruct them, "Quietly follow me."

I walk ahead, leading them away from the pathway, and toward another mountain range. I keep the group as close to the hillside as is possible, until there is no choice but to cross a grass filled expanse. I glance past the mountains with the villa, back to the distant hills, where my transport is, and cringe. We are moving farther and farther away, and to top that off, I do not even know if the power cell is going to be salvageable or functional.

Madcat limps toward me, then lays at my feet, and licks her paws. She tires easily these days, and the trek ahead promises to be a difficult one. I crouch down and stroke her head as I ponder the best course of action.

Natalie walks over to me and says, "Thank you for saving us. I know you could have left at any time."

I turn to her and reply, "I do not abandon…" I pause for a moment before finishing with, "my friends."

Natalie unexpectedly takes my hand in hers and with tears streaming down her face says, "My husband died defending us all, even you."

An unusual sensation runs up my spine as I realize that she is right. I was certainly the target of the attack, and as such all the guards had to do was to step aside, but instead they stood and defended the villa. I stare at her as it dawns on me that this group of people are truly loyal to me.

I lift my gaze to the wide expanse of grassland between us and the distant mountains, and then after a moment's reflection decide what to do. I pat Madcat as I issue my instructions, "Take my pet, and travel to the distant mountains. I will turn back and distract anyone who would follow you."

Madcat rises to follow me as I step away. Natalie gently grasps Madcat's fur behind her head and stops her. Madcat seems reluctant at first, but has come to trust Natalie, and after a moment, stops pulling away. Natalie coos soothingly as she leads my faithful companion.

I watch the ragtag group begin their long trek across the grassland, and then once I am certain that Madcat is staying with Natalie, I turn and sprint back toward the villa. I ignore the cave and make my way to the ramp up the hillside.

I slow down as I approach the base of the ramp and stay as close to the side of the steep hill as I can while being alert to the potential danger of lookouts. Movement from above catches my attention. I stop and focus on the motion. A troop of Royal Guards are marching down the hill, ignoring everything except the path they are on. I slink closer to the hillside and toward a narrow crevice, which I press into.

I watch out of the corner of my eye as about fifty guards march down the ramp. Once on the valley floor, they trudge toward the hills leading to the King's castle. I remain still until I am certain that none remain, and then cautiously make my way up the ramp. The guard post I built is in ruins, as is the villa itself. Faint wisps of smoke rise from the rubble, all that remains of the fine dwelling. The other smaller buildings have fared no better, and have either been burned to the ground, or smashed apart. The solar panels which were on every rooftop are now shattered remnants, and barely distinguishable for what they are.

I hurry toward the villa and begin to sift through the rubble. The sun is setting before I find the power cell. It is scorched and has a small dent in its casing. I cannot determine if it is functional, and even with my crafting tool, I am unable to properly test it. I turn toward the hills where my cave is, and then back to where Natalie and her group is headed. Though I am compelled to help her and Madcat, my survival instincts kick in.

I run as fast as I can toward the cave with the transport. I run through the night and arrive at my cave as the early rays of sunrise are creeping across the landscape. I remove as few boulders and rocks as is needed to allow myself to crawl inside. I make my way over the wall of rocks which conceal the shuttle and smile when I see the dust covered animal skins which cover the engine ports.

I enter the shuttle and power up its systems. Next I remove the animal skins, then test fire each of the thrusters. The main system reports ignition anomalies, but self corrects them in seconds. Finally, I connect the dented power cell, then hold my breath as I wait for the craft's systems to diagnose it.

"YES!" I shout gleefully; the report indicates the craft's total power is now at thirty-four percent.

I transfer the energy to the main power cell, and then leave the backup unit connected. Next I power everything down, and then cover the thruster ports. I am close to being able to launch. I check the status of the power coming from the solar collectors outside, and cringe at the negligible amount which trickles in. I grab a piece of cloth and make my way to the makeshift panels which are buried into the hillside.

The passage of time has caused these to fill with water, dirt, and silt, making them virtually useless. I shake my head as the obvious solution comes to mind, and immediately begin manufacturing the transparent dome cover for them. My crafting tool runs out of power before I am a quarter of the way done, so while it charges, I hunt and kill one of the grazing beasts.

The meat is delicious and reminds me of the food that Natalie would prepare. Thoughts of her and Madcat being in danger spur me into working faster, however due to the crafting tool's recharge time, progress is slow. During this time, I kill several more grazing beasts and prepare as much meat as is possible into food cubes. I also make a large backpack from the skins, and line the inside with a thin layer of insulation. Next, I individually seal the food cubes for long term storage, and pack them into the backpack. By the time I am done, I have a few weeks' supplies.

Finally, after three days, the protective dome is complete. I stand back and stare at my handiwork. The protective covering is sloped so that future rainfall will cause the dirt and rocks to skirt around, and not block the solar panels. Deciding that it will suffice, I turn my thoughts to Natalie's group. Knowing I will need to be rested for the long journey ahead, I sleep one last night in my pod, while recharging the crafting tool.

Waking refreshed, I quickly exit the pod and glance around as I run through a mental checklist of things to do. I confirm that the solar panels are providing energy, and even though it is a small amount, I am pleased. I shut down the rest of the craft's systems, leaving the recharging station operating. I place the crafting tool in one of the pouches on my belt, grab the backpack, which is filled with the preserved meat, and then step outside the cave. Next, I reseal the cave's entrance with rocks and dirt.

The morning is still early as I stare across the vast valley toward the hills where the destroyed villa is. I then look past them into the distance where Natalie's group is supposed to be hiding. The mountains are at least two days' travel, even for me. I take off at a comfortable lope, one intended to allow me to run for the extended length of time without tiring unduly.

I cross the creek, run past the woods, and then journey swiftly across the expanse of grassland toward the closer hills. Although I am making great time, the sun is casting long shadows as I pass the slope which leads to the villa. I continue my steady pace until I get to the cave where my secret passage exits. I slow my pace as I enter the cave.

Perhaps the long boring run has made me careless, or the fact that I see no signs of anyone; either way, the results are the same, I never see what strikes me from behind. As I lose consciousness it crosses my mind that I am not invincible. With blackness taking over, my final thoughts are of Madcat and Natalie.

Ensnared

"You're not so frightening now, are you?" A voice spits out with disdain.

I open my eyes and try to shake my head to clear the fuzziness but am held fast. I can feel the cold, sloping, surface that I am confined to. My head is held firm in a vice, with my arms spread straight out to either side. My legs are held slightly apart, with my feet suspended off the ground. I have a dull headache, and feel lethargic, as though I have been drugged. I attempt to focus on where I am but can only make out a distorted image.

A cold liquid of some sorts splashes across my face, and then runs down my chest and legs. The shock brings me to my senses, causing my scales to harden. My vision finally clears to reveal a man, dressed in fine armor, leaning over me. He makes a waving motion with his hand; almost immediately, I am swung vertically. My weight shifts, causing the metal clamps to bite into my arms and legs. I can feel them now, two per arm and leg, while a thick metal strap holds my head in place between two blocks of wood or metal.

The man slides a crate over, then stands on it to be eye level with me. He nods to someone out of sight as he says, "There is no escape for you this time, monster!"

The blocks on either side of my head are removed, allowing me to see a pair massive spikes, each of which is aimed at my armpits. Their length and size would drive them completely through me.

I stare at the man as I state, "So Jerry went back on his word, after all this time."

The man before me moves back and forth, clearly agitated, then replies, "My father was an idiot for helping you. He was weak! People knew about you, and yet he did nothing to protect us from you. But I…" he pauses as his anger threatens to overcome him, then he shouts out, "I had the courage to kill him, and now I will kill you."

I smile as it dawns on me who this man is. "You're the little boy from the villa. You were always scared of me."

The man shakes in fury and roars, "I'm scared of no one!" He steps down and rushes to my side where I can see him turning a wheel. I hear a clicking sound as the spikes slide closer. They touch my armpits, and then begin to press into them. The scales under my arms are soft and flexible, and unable to stop the spikes from penetrating. I feel blood trickle down my sides as the tips cruelly dig in.

The man stops turning the wheel, steps in front of me, and grins. He is breathing hard from his exertions. Sweat mats his hair and drips down his forehead onto his face. He motions to one side and barks, "Get this crap off me, I'm hot." Spittle flecks the side of his mouth as his rage continues.

Two men fearfully hurry to his side and begin to remove the man's armor.

This buys me the precious time I need. The pain has caused my scales to harden all over my body. As they toughen, they expand slightly, just enough to cause the tight-fitting metal clamps that hold me, to flex and buckle.

I strain hard against my tethers. Their snapping echoes loudly in the room. My next decision is tougher. In order to escape the spikes, I must drive one deeper into my body, to get the other out. The three men in the room stare at me, transfixed, as I slide to my left until my right side is free, and then with one last lunge, free my left side. Blood spurts out from under my left armpit, and my fingers tingle, indicating possible nerve damage. I spit out a gout of blood from a punctured lung, and then rush at the men, all of whom have drawn their swords.

The soldiers do their best to protect their liege, but their efforts are futile. One of the terrified men slashes weakly at me with his weapon, while the other lunges. I dodge the two attackers easily, and while keeping my left arm firmly held to my side, lash out with my right hand. In seconds I have severed one of the men's arms and ripped a bloody hole into the stomach of the other.

The man who tortured me is retreating toward the door. I grab him and hurl him viciously into the contraption I was held in. I bend the broken clasps over his arms and legs, digging the broken metal cruelly into his skin. His screams echo around the room as the metal bites into his flesh. I find the wheel that controls the spikes and turn it until the tips are pressed against his armpits.

"Stop, I will give you anything!" The man begs as tears flow down his face.

I stare at him and impassionedly state, "You are a waste of skin!"

He watches, wide eyed as I stuff a wad of material into his mouth to prevent his screams from being heard. I spin the wheel with a vengeance. The tips easily slice into his body, causing him to spasm violently as fright overtakes him. Blood gushes from the wounds, and then as I continue to turn the wheel, they penetrate deeper. I stop before they damage any major organs, and then leave him. I stare at the free-flowing blood and smile; he should bleed to death in a short time.

Froth bubbles from my nose due to my exertions, and my whole left side is streaked with blood. My right side is also bleeding, but nowhere near as much. I quickly examine the room and smile when I see my backpack and belt. Rummaging through the pouches on the belt, I find what remains of my medical kit. I open a small satchel, the last one of its kind, and then tip most of the powder into the hole under my left armpit. The rest I use on my right side. The powder stings, but the pain is not too great. I glance at the few crude tools and ignore them. Instead I stare at a small syringe, one labeled; 'single use', and the only one ever in the kit. I consider it for a moment, and then read the fine print, 'arterial repair nanites - experimental, use with caution.' I frown at the senseless warning. You either use it or not. I inject the contents into my left side, near the seeping wound, where the powder is already causing the blood to clot.

Lights dance before my eyes accompanied by a strange humming sound in my ears. My legs buckle, dropping me to the ground, where I lay in a semi-conscious state. A strange sensation flows from my left side, and spreads across my entire body. It is only now that I absentmindedly notice a patch of scales missing from my stomach. They appear to have been cut away, revealing the softer, replacement scales below.

The sensation passes, allowing me to stand once more. I turn to the man on the torture table and am surprised to see that he still clings to life. He is attempting to speak and succeeds in spitting the cloth out of his mouth.

"Please release me, I will give you anything." He weakly begs as his eyes flicker. He is pale from blood loss, and near death.

I leer at him as I state, "Were you ever told of my bargain with Jerry? I warned him that if he ever betrayed me, I would kill everyone he knew. Well, your betrayal shall cost you more."

I grab the wheel and spin it hard. The spikes drive completely through his body and exit out the other side. Blood pours from his mouth as he attempts to scream. The gurgling sounds of him drowning on his own blood as he dies are satisfying.

I take a deep breath and am surprised when both of my lungs function. The nanites seem to be working in conjunction with my own rapid healing process. I search the room for something to secure my left arm with. If I overexert myself and restart the bleeding, I do not have the means to heal myself anymore. I find a shield and use a piece of cloth from one of the dead soldier's tunics to tie it to my arm, and then pin my arm to my side. I grab one of the swords, open the door, and then stride out of the room.

A pair of guards' stare at me from down the dimly lit stone corridor, my door being the end room. Other doors line both sides of the passageway, but I have no interest in them. Instead I charge the two men, my heels leaving scratches in the stone floor as I propel myself forward. I cut them down before they can act.

A stone stairway leads upward from the small room they were in. As I walk to the steps, I notice a set of large keys hanging off a hook. The odds of my escaping would be enhanced by a distraction. I take the keys and starting with the furthest door from the stairway, I unlock each of them. Some of the stone cells have occupants, while others do not. All in all, I release twenty-two emaciated and filthy prisoners. They are in such poor physical condition it is difficult to tell who is male and who is female. Additionally, they are terrified beyond their senses when they see me and stay well away.

As I open the last door I turn to the group and state, "If you have any desire to live, you will fight, and escape." I shake my head at the ragtag group. They are no match for any soldier and would probably have lived longer had I left them confined.

The steady clomps of boots approach; at least two people are hurrying down the steps. I quickly drag the bodies of the dead guards out of sight and wait. The first man never sees the sword which decapitates him. The second man is still drawing his sword when I run mine completely through him, and then lift it up, severing cartilage and bone as I split his chest in two. The sword lodges in his body, where I leave it, for now.

Behind him are three more men, all staring, transfixed in terror. I take advantage of their hesitation, and leap at them. I grab the closest man's head and drive his skull into the wall so hard it cracks open like a melon. The wall is splattered with blood and brains as he tumbles lifelessly down the steps.

The two remaining guards' glance at each other, then flee up the stairs. I retrieve the sword, then bound after them; I cleave one across the back so viciously he is split from his shoulder to his buttocks, where my sword gets stuck again. I yank it out, toppling the lifeless body down the steps. His entrails snake after him as they slither down the stairwell. The last man is almost out of sight as he rounds the spiral staircase. I hurl the sword at him with all my might and miss. The sword strikes the wall beside him, and then, unbelievably, it ricochets into his side just as he rounds the bend. I charge up the steps to find the man sitting, slowly pulling the tip of the sword from his side. He clutches at the gaping and gushing wound as he attempts to back away from me. In a fit of rage, I drive my foot into his face. His nose and cheek bones shatter and cave in, as I use all my force. The man falls to the steps, and twitches as he dies.

I turn to the released prisoners to see them staring at the gory steps. As I retrieve my sword I bellow to the group, "Arm yourselves if you wish to live."

A few of the men reach for swords, then with renewed bravery, these few follow me up the stairwell. I climb cautiously, listening for sounds from above as I go.

I get to the top and see no one. A long wide stone corridor is before me. At the other end is a large door. On each side of the door is an ominous square hole. Suddenly an arrow flies from one of the holes, missing me by a mere fraction.

Thunk!

I turn at the sound and see one of the men who followed me toppling over. He is clutching at the arrow protruding from his chest. He hits the ground hard, driving his breath out in a bloody wheeze. His eyes roll as he dies.

Turning back to the door, I narrowly dodge an arrow, and then another. The men who were with me retreat back down the steps. I growl angrily, the door ahead is the only way out. I carry my sword in my near useless left hand, then pick up the body of the man with my right hand and sling him in front of me. Using the body, and my shield, as protection. I run at the door. Arriving, I toss the body down and am surprised to see three arrows sticking out of my thighs. I pluck them out, and hurl these to the ground as well.

As I had expected, I am too close to the door for those behind it to be able to fire at me. I chop at the door with my sword, keeping my aching left arm pressed to my side. It takes a while, but eventually I chip a piece of wood away. My own claws would be faster and more efficient but would put more stress on my injuries. The steady sound of me chipping away at the door has an unexpected effect. Someone on the inside opens it!

Six men charge out with raised swords. I hack at the first with my sword, driving it down through his collarbone, deep into his chest. I step backward as I attempt to pull the sword free. Its handgrip is slick with blood and slips from my hand. I lift my left arm a fraction and block a mighty blow from one of the attackers. I step back, narrowly avoiding a wild slash from another attacker. I drop to the ground and spin, lifting my foot as I do. My rearward claw slashes across the legs of three of the attackers, before I lose momentum.

Standing, I feel a fresh trickle of blood down my left side. My exertions are reopening the deep wound under my armpit. I charge at the remaining men, hacking and slashing with the claws of my right hand. They swing wildly at me, my scales blocking and deflecting most of the attacks. Seconds later they all lay at my feet, dead or dying. Black spots dance before my eyes. I shake my head to clear it, but only succeed in losing my balance and dropping to my knees.

As the edges of my vison become cloudy, I see two more attackers standing in the doorway. Surprisingly they do not attack, but instead flee. Unexpectedly, the prisoners I have released charge past me, and though they are obviously poorly skilled at swordsmanship, they are eager to escape, and fight with enthusiasm. The two guards dispatch three of them before they succumb to the sheer weight of numbers.

More rush past me, all except for one. A small, frail, boy leans to me and asks, "Are you okay Mister?"

I swallow blood as I reply, "I must get out of here."

The boy looks around, searching for something. He suddenly rushes off and returns moments later with a sturdy pole. Though he is weak, he helps me to my feet, then using the pole, I make my way through the doorway. I glance down and only then notice a huge gash across my chest, from which fresh blood freely flows. It seems that one of the soldiers succeeded in their attacks. I frown at an arrow which protrudes from my lower stomach. I rip it out, then feel a strange sensation as blood flows from the hole. The arrow was in deeper than I thought.

I stagger into the room and then lean against a large table. I rummage through the pouches, and then finding the only thing left is the construction tool, debate my options. It was never designed as a medical tool, but with little choice, I proceed. I turn it on and aim it at the gash in my chest. The pain is excruciating as I knit the wound together. The edges of my vision dim once more as I hesitantly aim it at my stomach.

I activate the unit and immediately let out an almighty howl. The crafting tool seals my seeping wound. The boy who is with me to steps back fearfully. My shriek echoes from the stone corridors behind, and to those ahead. I shut the tool off and close my eyes as consciousness threatens to abandon me. Swallowing hard, I open my eyes and stare at my handiwork, and am pleased to see that the bleeding has stopped. I hope the nanites I injected earlier are still in my blood stream, and able to repair my internal damage.

Staring at the doorway to freedom, I stumble toward it. The boy comes to my aid, helping as best he can. I wonder how the emancipated prisoners have been able to clear the area. Dead guards litter the corridors as the boy leads me outside.

The courtyard is a sight to behold. Bodies from both sides litter the ground. It is then that I realize what has happened. The prisoners released others, many others, before they attempted to escape.

I have little choice but to accept the boy's help as he leads me through the courtyard, and then finally outside the castle gates. Black dots dance before my eyes as consciousness once again threatens to leave me. I stagger down the path, letting the boy lead me to a grove of trees. When I can go no farther, I sit and then lean against a tree. I focus, first on breathing, and then on stemming the fresh blood which flows from more wounds than I knew I had.

I awake with a start, and stare around a panic. Three men are tending a fire, while a fourth is wrapping makeshift bandages over my wounds. The man bandaging my leg lifts his hands slowly as he stares fearfully into my eyes.

I hoarsely ask, "Why are you helping me?"

The man bandaging my leg points to the boy and says, "He insisted that we owe you our lives, and no matter how strange you are, that we should repay the debt."

"Gratitude." I reply weakly.

Another man walks toward me, carrying a steaming bowl. To my surprise he has cooked a meat and vegetable broth. I take the offering and devour the contents quickly.

The four men look around warily, then one of them states, "We must leave before the soldiers come from the main city."

I nod my head as I reply, "Thank you for your assistance." I point to the distant hills where Natalie and Madcat are supposed to be, and say, "My friends are there. Tell them Mamluk offered you sanctuary. They will understand and take you in."

I turn to the boy and say, "You should go with your people."

The boy stares at me and asks, "What about you?"

"I will leave this place and return to my people." The lie easily rolls off my tongue.

The boy reluctantly departs with the four men, leaving me alone. I am still leaning against the tree, covered in bandages. Once they are out of sight, I use the tree and a nearby pole to help me stand. I stare off into the distance and realize that there is nothing I can do for those I had promised to protect. My survival instincts kick in. I scarf down the rest of the broth, and then slowly head for my shuttle.

I lean heavily on the pole as I stagger along, occasionally stumbling as I go. The setting sun is casting long shadows across the grassland when I hear distant hoof beats. I turn and am alarmed to see how little distance I have covered. I focus on the noise and see a troop of five soldiers riding in my general direction. I cannot determine if they have seen me or not, and decide to crouch in the long grass, to watch them. Besides, I am unable to run, and the nearest cover is the same grove of trees I fled into many years ago, and too far away.

The riders are clearly in a hurry and push their beasts as they gallop along. I watch as they get closer and am relieved to see that they will not cross my position. The lead rider unexpectedly pulls his beast to a sliding halt, then begins to circle around.

He motions to the other riders as he says, "I tell you, that abomination does not live near the lava fields. It lives in the hills over there."

I watch with great concern as he points in the direction of my cave.

Another man, one who is having trouble controlling his beast, circles around as he replies, "Look, all I know is that we have to find it and kill it."

A third man jostles in his saddle as his beast snorts and stomps the ground. I suddenly realize that the beasts have picked up my scent, and that it is only a matter of time before the soldiers figure it out. I stare at the man who had pointed in the direction of my cave, and decide that he must die, even if the others escape.

I stand up and shout, "I live in these fields, you fools!"

The beasts panic. Two dump their riders and take off at high speed. The rest of the men get down from their animals before they are thrown off, and then with swords raised, cautiously approach me.

The soldiers work together to surround me, and yet they also keep their distance, as if they know of my capabilities. The five men glance warily at each other, and then step closer. I stand my ground, and then take a few deep breaths as I wait for the inevitable combat. Many of my scales harden as my adrenaline flows, but many do not. Worse still, I am no longer able to lift my left arm.

I lean heavily on the pole, and then lower my head, as if exhausted, which is not too far from the truth. As expected, they all rush at me. I lift the pole and then instead of parrying with it, ram it into the face of the man who had pointed in the direction of my shuttle. The end of the pole drives the man's nose into his face, killing him almost instantly.

I pull the pole back and quickly spin to one side, narrowly avoiding a sword thrust which skims across the scales on my chest, leaving a narrow groove as it passes. Another swings his sword down in a powerful arc, one intended to cleave into my shoulder. I drop down, and to one side, as I lift the pole. I drive the blunt pole under his chin, and shove with all the strength my right arm can muster. Surprisingly, the pole breaks through his skin, and then penetrates all the way through, until it hits the inside of his skull, where it stops. I use so much force, the impaled man is lifted from the ground, and for a moment, spasms wildly on the pole as he dies.

I roar in pain as a sword is thrust into my back. Letting go of the pole, I lurch forward, before the sword can be driven in too deep, only to come face to face with another sword wielding soldier. He grins as he thrusts his weapon at my face. In desperation I dive to the ground and roll to one side. I kick out with both feet as I attempt to avoid the weapons. My breathing is labored as I get to my feet. Only two men face me, it would seem my wild kick injured one of the others.

The two remaining men look at their injured colleague, then grab him and drag him back. His knees are bent like mine, which is the wrong way for his species.

I point at them and state far more confidently than I feel, "I will let you live this day, but forever tell your children to avoid this area, or I will kill them and eat them."

The men stare at me fearfully. As far as they are concerned, I am invincible. The two able bodied men call after their mounts, and then chase them down. Once they finally have them, they flee with their injured comrade.

I retrieve the pole, which is still firmly stuck in the soldier's head, then turn to the distant hills where my shuttle rests. Summoning all my willpower, I continue my long trek. I attempt to stem the flow of blood from my back, but merely succeed in slowing it down to a trickle. All through the night I stagger, ever onwards.

The following day is a blur as I mechanically place one foot in front of the other. By the end of the day I can see the creek which flows near my cave. I reach the flowing water, and falling into it, drink deeply to quench my thirst. I feel energy returning to my muscles but must muster all my remaining strength to resist the urge to fall asleep where I lay.

I rise, wade across the water, and make my way toward my cave. Before I attempt to enter, I look back at the way I have come, and grin. Despite my injuries, I have made it. I stagger toward the cave's blocked entry way, and carefully clear as little as possible to allow me access. I crawl through the narrow passageway and take the time needed to seal it behind me as I go.

With the last of my energy sapped, I make my way to the rock wall that hides my shuttle, and painstakingly climb over it. No longer able to stand, I crawl into the shuttle, then using the control panels, get to my feet. I activate my pod, then teeter my way to it. I remove the bandages, then step back into the pod. I close my eyes as the lid closes, and immediately lose consciousness.

Chapter Four – War

I am suddenly awakened as I am violently tossed from my pod. I shake my dazed head, and stand. Quickly checking the pod, I can see no obvious signs of damage, and am grateful the covering slid back prior to my being ejected. I stagger on my feet and am having trouble focusing my thoughts. Parched, and ravenously hungry from hibernating, I gulp down copious amounts of water to rehydrate, and then eat an entire ration pack, all in a matter of minutes. Though I am sated, I find it odd that the food and water taste stale.

As my mind clears, I recall why I entered the pod, and quickly examine my wounds. I am pleased to see that all that remains of them is a few scars. I stare at my marred scales and frown. My damaged scales should have flaked off, leaving fresh ones in their place. I put this out of mind as I clear a thick layer of dust off the pilot's panel. Checking the transport's power levels provides me with some good news. There is almost enough to launch off the planet. How the shuttle gained energy while running the pod, baffles me. I check the craft's statistics and stare in disbelief at the readings. According to the computer, I have been asleep for hundreds of years. No wonder the main power cell has the reserves it does. The fact that it is still receiving a trickle of power, is testimony to the Protectorate's technology.

A powerful blast rattles the cave and causes dirt to fall from the ceiling. A few rocks shift and fall from my makeshift wall. I stare through the dust filled air and wonder if this is the reason I was roused from my slumber. I stare at the shuttle and realize that I need to find out what is going on before conducting any systems tests.

I make my way to where I sealed the cave, and warily clear the way. Whatever is going on outside, it is causing dirt to fall from the ceiling in ever increasing clouds. I finally step outside and take in my surroundings. Where the creek once meandered, now a river of lava flows. The grassland on either side is covered in ash, and residual lava. I turn my gaze to the lava's source and stare in surprise at the distant volcano that has sprung from the ground during my slumber.

A howling sound approaches, then passes overhead. A distant thud followed by a massive explosion shakes the landscape. Rocks and shale rain down from the top of the mountain. I turn, then stare at where my solar collector should be, and frown. The area is unrecognizable. I climb the hill, and after a brief search, find it. Amazingly, it is still intact, and has been well shielded by the rocky outcropping above it.

While I deliberate the best course of action, another howling sound approaches. I stare at the mountains on the far side of the valley, searching for the source of the noise. I notice what appear to be gigantic guns lining the distant mountain range, one just past the old villa, and where I sent Madcat and Natalie. The guns are firing massive projectiles toward the top of the mountain my cave is in. Each shell that strikes showers the area with rocks and pebbles. I hurriedly disconnect the solar unit and make a few trips to my cave with the various components. I place the solar unit pieces inside the shuttle, then return outside.

A series of deafening explosions blast from the top of the mountain. Dozens of enormous projectiles streak toward the distant mountain peak. I watch, fascinated, as they strike, the impact sending great gouts of dirt into the air. None of the impacts seem to hit any of the opponent's weapons.

I sigh. It is clear that both sides have achieved a stalemate. Even if one side were to damage, or destroy the other, the lava would seem to be preventing the winners from capitalizing on their advantage.

I have no idea why the two sides are warring, and nor do I care. With the safety of my transport being my primary concern, I begin the long climb to the top of my mountain.

Climbing with deliberate care, I seek shelter as each volley of shells approach. Every impact leaves a massive crater and hurtles great chunks of dirt and rock into the air. One impact occurs so close to me the rock I am crouched behind cracks from the force of the explosion.

Eventually, I arrive at the ridge line, and stare in astonishment at the mechanical monstrosities before me. The gun barrels that extend over the mountain top are but a bare fraction of the weapon's size. The entire far side of the mountain has been altered drastically. Huge roadways line the valley floor, along with a railway. The valley floor is littered with supply depots, while the hills on the far side are speckled with impact craters from projectiles which have overshot their mark.

I stare in wonder at the number of cannons. More than fifty line the mountain top, stretching into the distance as far as I can see. Long conveyors transport munitions up the mountain to staging areas at the base of each weapon. Another road snakes its way along the mountainside, connecting each of these staging areas.

Each cannon is a hive of activity. I watch as a group loads a single massive shell into slots in a vertical chain. I can hear the weapon's inner workings moving as the shell is lifted. The cannon unexpectedly thunders, launching an artillery shell over the lava, and at the distant mountain top. While keeping out of sight, I move to get a clearer view. I am stunned at the basic nature of the weapon. The massive chain runs from the base of the cannon, to its firing chamber. I can see fifteen shells between the loading area and rear section of the cannon. The chain stops, the cannon roars, then the chain moves once more. The loading crews use the brief time the chain is stopped to load a new shell.

The sound of a whistle blowing loudly interrupts my thoughts. I turn to see a long train meandering its way along the valley floor. It is heavily laden with covered cars. I wait and watch as the train stops and is then unloaded. Many of the carriages carry fresh shells, while others are filled to the brim with rocks. These rocks are transported to dozens of small buildings on the valley floor.

I stare at the buildings, attempting to figure out what they are. I hear distant clangs and hisses as a wide door to one of these buildings is opened. I grin at the realization that these are small power stations, designed to operate the cannons, and perhaps more.

I stare at the weapons, and then realize that I need to stop the fighting. I frown as the shrill howl of an incoming artillery shell approaches. It impacts three weapons away and is a direct hit on the cannon. The weapon explodes spectacularly; its entire upper workings are thrown clear across the valley. Its chain, still filled with unfired shells, falls. The loading crew attempts to escape. The shell filled chain lands on the roadway, then slides over the edge and skids down the steep slope to the valley floor.

I expect the unfired shells to explode upon impact, yet they do not. Minutes later a fleet of repair crews arrive. They take the unused shells toward the cannons on either side, and then begin clearing the debris. I then notice that many of the cannons, that I thought were functional, are not. This explains the sporadic firing, but what of their opponents?

I also wonder why I had not been woken up earlier than I was. It is clear these cannons have been in existence for quite some time. I finally notice what may have woken me. One of the large doors that leads to what I surmise is small power station, opens. Acrid smoke pours from the door, as do dozens of people who stagger out. Many of these stumble away from the door, while others collapse where they are. Either an accident or sabotage has blown up one of their power stations.

BOOM!

I grab the nearest rock to steady myself as the mountain shudders. Rocks avalanche down both slopes in great sheets. A massive cloud of dust rises from the valley floor obscuring my view of the area. Unexpectedly, an object whistles past my head, and impales itself into the ground behind me. I shake my head to clear the ringing from yet another powerful blast, and then quickly seek the shelter of a boulder as shrapnel flies out in all directions. I stay crouched down as explosion after explosion rips through the air.

Finally, I lift my head and examine the area. The train's engine looks as though some great thing burst its way out of its boiler. The tracks beneath it are a twisted ruined mess. The trains last few carriages lay on their sides, violently ripped from their couplings.

Almost all the staging areas are gone, replaced by the twisted remains of the powerful cannons. Glancing up and down the ridge line, I can see only five cannons which seem to be intact. None of these will have ammunition for long, not with their supply system in tatters. A strange sound assaults my ears through the ringing. I stare down at the valley, toward the noise, and see a great force of armored vehicles heading my way.

I watch with fascination as the approaching military forces attack those in the valley, killing all. I lift my gaze and frown. Far in the distance, smoke billows into the air in huge dark clouds. It seems I have woken up to witness the end of a war. Staring at remnants of the battlefield, an idea comes to mind. I may be able to use one of the mini power plants, if they do not destroy them all, to charge my craft even more.

With little to do except wait for the forces to leave, my thoughts drift. I wonder about the planet's current technology. My curiosity eventually gets the better of me. I keep myself well concealed as I make my way toward the smoke. I spend the night curled up in a hillside crater, well away from any paths.

I wake early, and stare at the stars for a moment. A sense of dread fills me when I realize that many of the sparkles in the night are probably the Protectorate's deep space facilities. I stare at the specks of light for a few minutes, then putting all thoughts of space from my mind, continue my trek. The ridgeline is providing less and less cover, and what was an occasional military vehicle, is now an almost non-stop parade of them.

I am about to quit my trek, and return to my cave, when a strange wailing sound assaults my ears. I turn to its source, the rising smoke, and wait curiously. The strange noise changes in pitch, rising and falling rhythmically. A large number of ground vehicles drive along the valley where the train tracks are. They are in such a hurry that no one pays me any attention. Instead of the orderly groups as before, there is now a flurry of chaotic activity as vehicles race along at high speeds. I hear voices calling out in fear, and then I hear two words which send a chill through my body, "Energy bomb!"

Almost immediately I notice a distant object in the sky, one which slowly approaches. I focus on it intently, and can see that it is a huge airship, propelled by gigantic blades. Beneath its main body, cradled in a large frame, rests a metallic object.

I turn and run, ignoring the fact that I may be spotted. How the hell this backward planet has developed what appears to an atomic-type weapon is beyond my comprehension. My clawed heels dig huge holes as I sprint as fast as I can to get as much of the hill between me and the expected blast as possible.

I see the glow ahead of me before I feel the change in air pressure or hear the sound. I dive for a depression and curl up in a tight ball. The blast is insanely powerful, and deafening. Massive chunks of the hilltop are blown down onto me, adding to my cover. A heatwave of unimaginable power rushes past me, and then subsides. Behind me, the airship is engulfed in the furies it has unleashed. It falls from the sky, and crashes into the ruins of the city.

I lay still for many minutes, waiting. Finally, I stand and brush dirt and rocks off my body. I glance at the blackened landscape, and the distant mushroom cloud, then turn toward my cave, and run. I maintain a good pace as I traverse the rocky landscape.

Unexpectedly, something strikes my right shoulder, then as I turn, a small object hits my chest. I stare at the hole in my scales with incredulity. I lift my gaze and see a man holding a firearm. He drops his weapon, and flees, clearly terrified. I stare at the superficial wound in my chest with indifference, then, being mindful of other survivors, I continue on my way, paying greater attention to my surroundings.

I do not see anyone else during my return journey, and once inside my cave, I enter the shuttle and activate my pod's medical scanner. I step inside and wait for the unit to complete its cycle. Stepping out and checking the analysis provides me with some much-needed relief. The residual radiation in my body is negligible, and from an extremely rare element. It seems that I am either immune to it, or I got extremely lucky. I grab the first aid kit and remove both projectiles. The one in my chest is easy to get to, while the projectile that is in my shoulder, proves to be quite difficult. Eventually I have both metallic nuggets out. I wonder at the planet's varying technology. One side is using projectile weaponry, the other, atomic-like weapons. With such a disparity, the outcome is clear.

I suddenly realize that I have a small radiation scanner as part of the shuttle's standard equipment. I activate it, then watch as the readings climb into the caution zone. I make my way outside and over the ridgeline to the valley behind my cave. The radiation is higher, but still far from the scanner's danger zone.

Gazing down at the valley floor I see the ground is littered with debris and bodies. I stare at the dozens of doorways, most of which are smoke stained, and consider my options. I select one that seems undamaged, make my way to it, and enter.

Lights flicker along the ceiling of a corridor that stretches deep into the mountain. Water or blood, pools on the concrete floor. I cautiously make my way down the passageway. At around two hundred paces, another doorway blocks my path. The double doors are unlocked, and open inward with ease. I step into a large room, its lights also flicker randomly, I quickly inspect the area.

The room appears to be a control center. I notice an area where fuel is loaded into a furnace, and another location which has a massive panel. I examine the control board at length, and then close my eyes as I imagine the small power plant's process. It is basically a steam powered generator. The fuel source is a compressed material which burns for a lengthy period of time. I easy locate the bricks of fuel, and the archaic system of loading them. A person literally opens the furnace doors, tosses in a brick, and then closes the doors.

I consider numerous ways of automating this process. I finally decide that no matter what I do, the main issue is harnessing the power. I would have to connect the generator's crude output into my shuttle's power grid. I have no way of measuring the plant's power output, and although I am certain it is low, I am not going to risk blowing the shuttle's circuits. Ironically, I need a more advanced technology, one with metered output. Standing right next to a power source that could provide me with an abundance of energy, or leave me permanently marooned, is frustrating.

I glance at the radiation scanner, and then decide to satisfy my curiosity about the city destroyed by the bomb. I step outside and examine the few ground vehicles in the area. I stare at the hand and foot controls and the seats which again my legs will not allow me to sit upon. I rip a seat out of one of the vehicles but am unable to figure out how to start its engine.

I stare at the basic controls, and then consider who would be operating it. There is one-foot pedal, a large steering wheel, and a series of knobs on a panel that faces the driver. A wide window affords an unobstructed view ahead. Nothing I touch, turn, or press, starts the vehicle's engine. Eventually I have no choice but to give up and begin the trek to the source of the explosion on foot.

I look at my radiation scanner once more and frown. It still registers in the caution zone, which means that the atomic-like bomb was either a low yield variety with a short half-life, or the radiation spectrum is not detectible. I consider turning back, but instead, decide to put my faith in the technology. If I have learned anything from my training sessions, it is that the Protectorate prides itself on its scientific achievements.

The closer I get to the source of the detonation; the more carnage I witness. It then dawns on me that whoever used the bomb eliminated the residents of the city, and based on the colored markings, the military units of two differing factions. I wonder if there is a third party in the war. Usually, hostilities are between only two sides.

I round a bend and stop. There before me, rests the remains of a sprawling city. It is difficult to judge how high the tallest buildings were, but my best guess is that they were at least eight stories high. Most of the area is devastated, but many of the older, stone buildings remain relatively intact. I make my way to the largest of these, stepping over and around a growing number of shriveled corpses. If there were any survivors, they have long since left.

The city shows signs of having a rudimentary power grid, which is now destroyed and lays in tatters along the sides of the wide streets. Scorched and burned vehicles line the roads, many with their occupants still inside, grotesquely killed by the powerful energies unleashed by the weapon.

I climb the steps to the large building, and then enter through its thick double doors. The wood is charred, but as the entrance faces away from the source of the explosion, they were spared the direct blast. The foyer is quite large, and leads to a main room, which has at its centerpiece, an enormous skeleton of some large creature I have never seen before. Though the room is dark, my eyes can easily discern everything around me. The walls are lined with paintings depicting various strange creatures and scenes. Dozens of corridors radiate off this room, while a wide stairwell leads to a second level. I stare at a plaque on the wall near me, and slowly read its engraved words. "Historical Library."

It takes me a moment, but finally I realize that this is a museum. I stare at the plaque in awe. I had no idea that I could read the local language and wonder if this knowledge was gleaned from my pod, or if I have an innate ability to read. I frown as I realize that I had trouble deciphering the power plant's functions. I put the thought away, and gaze at my surroundings.

I casually walk down one of the corridors and stare at numerous displays, each of which depicts a different time in the planet's history. Another corridor is dedicated to small creatures, while yet another displays images of various plants and trees. I take my time, slowly reading all I can. The more I read, the easier it becomes.

Making my way down yet another corridor I stare at a series of outlandish images depicting strange looking creatures. The blood drains from my face when I realize that these are crude depictions of me. I turn to leave and come face to face with a large pelt that adorns a wall. A caption beneath it reads; 'This is the beast that terrorized the local mountains, killing hundreds during its reign of terror.'

I stare at the pelt for a moment, and then gingerly pat the scar that would have been on Madcat's chest. I remain there for some time, memorizing the five names that adorn the plaque below the pelt. I leave the building, somewhat perplexed by why Madcat's death bothers me. I have cleaved and killed hundreds, and their deaths meant nothing to me. I stare dispassionately at the desolation around me. I feel nothing for the people who died here, and yet the death of that animal at the hands of someone, is another matter completely.

I roar loudly at the sky in anguish. My craving for revenge is almost as great as my longing to leave this wretched planet.

With a heavy heart I make my way back to my cave. The artillery fire from both sides has stopped; I have no way to tell, but perhaps the war is over. I make my way to the shuttle where I begin preparations to leave.

Before I clear the cave's entrance, I test all the shuttle's systems, and not just the thrusters. I stare at a readout in disbelief, and almost slam my fist into the console in frustration. Now that the craft has enough power to launch, it will not. I stare at the password request brought up by activating the launch protocol, and growl in anger. The hull breach of so long ago tripped a safety feature, one that now requires an override code to clear.

I frown in confusion as the computer system that requires the code, begins to run a password cracking utility. I stare at the utility and then smile. The computer is attempting to hack its own password. There is no way that this feature is part of the shuttle's standard software package.

I have no idea how long the task will take, so with a devilish grin, I decide that fate is allowing me to seek out Madcat's killers. Even though the actual persons may be dead, their linage may yet prevail, but not for long. To find the people will require information, and I think I know just where I will find it.

Revenge

I exit my cave and climb over the mountain. I cautiously approach the entrance to the power station I had explored earlier. I listen carefully before proceeding to the control room. Once there, I search for a computer, but all I find are crude systems which have limited functionality.

I am about abandon my search, when an object catches my attention. It is a large pile of papers, bound with a cover of sorts. It is slightly damaged with numerous dog-eared corners, as if from much use. I pick it up, open it, and stare in disbelief at the lists of names, along with numbers, and what appears to be locations.

I skim through the pages and quickly determine that they are sorted alphabetically, by the person's last name. The first name from the plaque results in seven pages of possible locations. The second name has fewer than a dozen possibilities. I tear out each page that is relevant, ending up with almost twenty in all.

It then dawns on me that I have no idea which of the names belongs to the linage that is ultimately responsible, nor do I know how to find them. I skim through the pages, searching for anything that could help me figure out who I should confront. When nothing I review helps, I fold the pages, and put them in a pouch.

Frustration builds again. I have list of people which even includes their residences, but I have no way of knowing where these locations are. If only I had a recent planetary scan, or access to a database.

My desire for revenge is high, but not at the cost of my own life, and to date there have been a couple of close calls. I spend a few moments weighing my options, and then thoroughly search the area once more. Finding nothing that will help me, I stop and consider the technology around me. The lack of computer systems, and the seemingly heavy usage of paper for information is perplexing to me. Some regions of this planet are clearly a five on the Technology Index, while others, based on the usage of cannons, are still a four. How these factions waged war is as baffling as is my dilemma.

I leave the power station, and then stare at the carnage in the valley. The train is a shredded ruin, while most of the massive cannons that line the mountainside are piles of twisted metal. Many of the vehicles in the valley are obviously damaged, some even on their sides. The vehicle I inspected earlier still rests upright, exactly as I left it.

I stare at it as something clicks in my mind. The operators must know where to go, and if they do not have computers, how do they know? My fingers absentmindedly tap the pouch with the papers in it. I stop and stare at the pouch as it dawns on me, paper maps!

I hurry to the vehicle, then begin opening every compartment I can see. I easily find what I am looking for. A large manuscript with a colored top page depicting a crisscross of lines stares at me. I take it out and examine it. The locations on the torn-out pages are easily found once I figure out the map's indexing. I smile as I flick to the back, and find continental, regional, and local maps. I retire to the shuttle and begin forming a list.

By nightfall I not only have a list of nearly one hundred eighty addresses, I have sorted them as I would a search grid, extending out in a radius from where Madcat's pelt was hung. I factor in the mountain range where she and Natalie were supposed be hiding, which gives me an oval shaped area to reconnoiter. My first task, however, is to determine if Natalie survived, and if she had any offspring. This is complicated by the fact that I do not know her last name.

Knowing how this planet's people store their data makes my task easier. My first stop will be at a records building, or a historical library, and thanks to the comprehensive index in the front of the book of maps I found, I have marked many possibilities. I ignore the city, which was destroyed by the powerful blast, and instead focus on the old castle, which is marked as a historical preserve, and according to the maps, contains a massive library.

I am about to leave the shuttle when I am thunderstruck by an idea. I hurry to the shuttle's pilot station and activate the communications system. I then filter the thousands of transmissions received, down to those in the area I have marked on my maps. I sit and listen, flicking from one frequency to another, until I finally find what I am looking for. An encrypted military channel, one the shuttle's systems has no trouble deciphering. I glance at the password cracking tool and see that it is still running and return my attention to the transmissions.

Listening to the military channel tells me what I had already suspected, the war is indeed over. In addition, the entire region around the devastated city is to be evacuated, with the surviving inhabitants to be relocated far away. The surrendered military forces are being taken to holding areas where the victorious side plans to debrief anyone of importance. It seems they will be allowed to return to their homes once they have been processed. I find this odd; I would eliminate the losers, to prevent any future uprisings. The victorious faction is also establishing a presence in the conquered region as quickly as they can.

I continue to listen, until I get my final answer; there are three opposing sides in the war. Two of which are at similar technological levels, with the third being more advanced. It would seem the advanced party had warned of committing acts of mass destruction if the warring factions did not come to some agreement. The bomb was a demonstration of that ability. I also hear messages of retaliation, of planned assassinations, and acts of terrorism. The names and places listed are quite extensive.

With all the activity going on, I expect the few roads and bridges will be quite busy. Alarmingly, the maps indicate only one bridge across the lava flow, and not only is it quite a distance away, someone has drawn a strange symbol on the map over it. I do not know what the symbol means, but based on the transmissions, the bridge is in heavy use, and thus, still intact.

I consider crossing the lava by some other means, but the time it would take to craft a makeshift bridge would be better spent travelling. Besides, the less I do to draw attention to myself, the better.

I step outside with a clear plan in mind and stop. A colossal airship is hovering over the field on the far side of the lava. Beneath it is a huge metallic container, one that is being lowered to the ground. The second the object reaches the ground, one side opens, and disgorges dozens of military personal, along with a pair of ground vehicles. Two more air ships of equal size are approaching from the distance. I crouch down and watch as the cargo of all three airships is unloaded.

Though their proximity to my cave is slightly disconcerting, it is clear the forces are simply attempting to assemble a bridge over the lava. I look up and down the valley and wonder why they are going to so much trouble. There are no roads on either side, and it is clear the airships could have transported their cargo virtually anywhere.

I rise and am about to leave when the rumble of engines reaches my ears. I tilt my head and listen intently. A distant dust cloud reveals the source of the noise, and the reason for the bridges, hundreds of ground vehicles are approaching. I glance around warily. If I do not leave soon, I may not be able to. Keeping low to the rocks, I follow the flowing lava in the direction of the devastated city, and the bridge.

The lava follows the contours of the land, and soon angles away from the city, into a deep ravine. In the distance I find what I have been hoping for. An intact bridge. As I approach, I notice that its metal frame is buckled and twisted, and yet I see ground vehicles crossing it. Stationed on either side of the bridge, are a handful of armed guards. I examine the bridge intently, then decide that I can either attempt to cross it by making my way along the frame underneath the roadway, or I can hide myself in one of the large trucks.

Moving toward the road, I see that it is as black as my scales, and smooth, with a single white line painted down the center. I grin when I see piles of rocks and boulders near the road's edge. I crouch down behind the largest pile and wait. Moments later a convoy of vehicles approaches, and they are heading in the right direction. I stay hidden as they pass and wait for the last vehicle with nervous anticipation. Lucky for me, it has a large covered trailer that my thermal vision shows as empty. I glance at the cabin area as it passes. If the operator notices me, then I will have little choice but to flee. I roll toward the rear of the truck, then jump onto the back. There are few handholds, and out of pure reflex, my claws penetrate the rear doors as I attempt to hold on. I dig long vertical grooves right through the thin metal sheet, until my slow fall is arrested.

I hurriedly open one side and climb in. I shut the door just as the truck approaches a group of guards. I am alarmed when the vehicle slows, but moments later we accelerate across the bridge, relieving my momentary concern. I stare at the light that shines through the grooves made by my claws. Peeking through the largest hole, I am relieved when I see none of the guards paying the truck any attention.

I am jostled as the truck bounces its way across the bridge, and past another group of equally apathetic guards. Staring through the grooves, I notice that the road shows signs of many repairs, and as we bounce along, it is obvious that more are needed. I wait until I am well away from the bridge before I open the rear door. I let it swing free, then cringe as I realize the driver may see the swinging door. Indeed, seconds later the truck slows, and then stops.

I quickly glance at my surroundings then, seeing that it is clear, jump to the ground and roll to a stop. I lay flat on my stomach, and observe a person walking alongside the vehicle. I quickly stand, then sprint in the opposite direction. I dive behind some light brush just as the man rounds the corner of the truck. Fortunately, he is staring at the swinging door, thus my escape goes unnoticed. I watch as the man scratches his head, then shuts the truck's door. He stares at the grooves, then glances around warily. Suddenly he runs back to the front of the vehicle and jumps into the cabin. The vehicle's engine protests loudly, harsh grinding sounds accompany each lurch the truck makes as it gathers speed and accelerates away.

I quickly gather my surroundings, then frown; the ravine, with its tall cliff faces on either side, feels oddly familiar. It suddenly dawns on me that this is the ravine where I caused the rockslides so long ago, and when I killed the king, allowing Jerry to assume the mantel. I glance ahead, and behind, but the curves prevent me from seeing any great distance.

If my memory serves me, I should find a road leading up the hill to the old castle. The rumble of distant engines reaches my ears. I glance apprehensively up and down the ravine. The reverberating noise echoes from the walls, making it difficult to determine which way the trucks are coming from. I decide to sprint away from the bridge, hoping to find the way to the castle before the approaching vehicles can see me.

Today is my lucky day. As I run alongside the smooth roadway, I can hear that the approaching vehicles are behind me. In addition, I soon come upon a stone paved road leading up the hill, and out of the ravine. A sign which reads, 'Historical Preserve', dominates the corner of the two roadways. I sprint up the hill, alongside the stones just as a truck rounds the bend. I find a decent sized nook, and back into it, then wait. Mere seconds later, the lead vehicle of what sounds like a large convoy, rumbles past the side road. I wait and watch as more than twenty trucks pass by.

Once the coast is clear, I begin my climb up the hill. I do not recall the paved stones, nor the way the road winds its way up the hillside. Picturesque signs along the way detail some of the castle's basic facts, such as, when it was built, and by who. The signs also indicate the castle's size, and include the materials used in its construction. I read all the signs out of curiosity as I plod my way along the cobblestone road.

It would seem the entire area is vacant of any people, and as an added bonus, shows no signs of damage from the war. I arrive at a closed pair of massive gates, which are nestled into a tall and sturdy looking stone wall. A simple sign reads, 'Closed, by order of the Imperium'

I wonder who the Imperium is and consider the title with amusement. This planet has no idea what an empire truly is. At that thought, I glance at the stars and consider the Atlan Protectorate's vast domain, and its trillions of inhabitants. The pod has provided me with a wealth of knowledge, including information never intended for my kind. I return my thoughts to the simple gates, and easily bypass its crude security locks.

Swinging the gates open and stepping into the courtyard brings back memories. Surprisingly, much of the castle appears as it did when I last saw it. There are a few minor additions, but nothing extensive. I decide to follow a series of arrows, which according to the signs, are a self-guided tour.

As I walk casually from one room to another, I begin to make sense of the castle's history. This fills in the massive blank left by my long slumber. I come to a great room and stop and stare at the startling sight before me. A massive statue dominates the center of the room. One that depicts Natalie riding astride Madcat. I stare up at the larger than life depiction of my old faithful companion and feel a sense of pride. Whoever crafted the statue even included the scar on her chest. Something in Natalie's hand grabs my attention. I walk around to get a clearer view, and then see that she holds a small object which seems oddly like my crafting tool. I shake my head in wonder. Whoever crafted the amazing statue got many details correct, and yet Natalie never rode Madcat.

I read depiction after depiction and then feel a chill run up my spine. All the pieces begin to fall into place. The few surviving members of the royal family rebuilt their kingdom around this very castle. They pursued, and successfully drove Natalie, and the other survivors from the villa, away from the mountains, killing Madcat in the process.

Natalie and her small group of survivors salvaged the solar panels, and over time her group reverse engineered them, providing them a massive advantage over the rest of the planet. They eventually retreated to a distant island chain, and then kept to themselves for many years. Anyone wishing to join them simply had to swear allegiance to the Imperium, the name they gave themselves. Over the years they grew and built a series of magnificent cities. These cities easily repelled any attackers, and quickly gained a reputation of being impregnable. I gulp as I realize that these people were able to create electrical circuits and solar panels while the rest of the planet was still struggling with steam power.

The roving bandits eventually formed their own group, and soon went to war against their neighbors. These petty conflicts persisted for years, until two factions eventually formed. These two sides became embroiled in a bitter war, one the Imperium kept out of, until recently.

In an attempt to gain the Imperium's favor, this castle was deemed a historical preserve and the monument to Natalie and Madcat was commissioned. The other faction decided to counter this effort and hung Madcat's pelt in what they thought was a sign of respect and honor.

The Imperium saw the growing death toll from the unrelenting conflict and decided to send their own message. By destroying the city displaying Madcat's pelt, they let both sides know that they would not be placated so easily. Now they are sending conventional looking weaponry to maintain a presence, thus enforcing the peace.

My head snaps up as something else falls into place. One of the factions is planning to assassinate a prominent member of the Imperium and, if I recall correctly, they have a suicide squad in place. The name matches one of those I read somewhere around here, and something about that name nags at me as being important. I just cannot recall what. I hurry from placard to placard until I am finally staring at one in the main room with the large statue. "In honor of Clive Yanko, the last of Natalie's descendants."

Staring at the statue, I state solemnly, "I could not protect you, but I shall try to save your linage."

I consider what I have learned, and then using the various maps that adorn many of the displays, I form a plan. The capital city where Clive lives, is a long way off. Fortunately, the roadway below is one of many that lead to it. There are only a few bridge systems that cross the islands, and a single tunnel, which I immediately rule out as being far too risky. I have no intentions of being trapped in an underwater tunnel.

With my mind made up, I make my way back to the road which runs through the valley. As expected, there is not a soul in sight, making the trek down the hill an easy one. I arrive at the bottom, and then look around for a place to hide. A short distance away is a large pile of boulders, near some shrubs. I glance all around, and then still seeing no one, hurry to the rocks. I crouch down behind them and wait.

Only a short time passes before the unmistakable sound of an engine approaches, and it is going in the direction I need. I glance through the foliage, then sigh. It is an open vehicle, filled with passengers. I relax back against the rocks and wait. Each time I hear engines, I assess them, and then continue to wait, biding my time. There are regular convoys of vehicles, some with passengers, and some with various unidentifiable cargo.

My patience is finally rewarded. The perfect convoy trundles slowly past, giving me ample opportunity to sneak aboard the last truck; it is partially filled with cargo. Once inside, I claw out a small peep hole in the back door, and then rest on a large wooden box and wait once more. The journey is quite lengthy. Every now and then, I hear vehicles travelling in the opposite direction.

Taking occasional peeks through the hole lets me keep my bearings. I remain hidden all the way to the border region where the bridges start and decide to abandon my ride. Fortunately, the vehicles that caught up to the slow-moving convoy either overtook us or turned onto side roads.

With the traffic becoming more frequent, I wait for a lull in the noise. As soon as I get my chance, I carefully open the rear door, and jump. No sooner do I hit the ground and roll; I hear a vehicle approaching from the opposite direction. I dive for the side of the road, and then slide down the unexpected, and steep, embankment. I land at the bottom of the hill amid a shower of pebbles and small stones. I watch the top of the hill, almost expecting someone to see me. As the seconds tick by, and it seems my escape is unnoticed, I relax.

I stare across the wide expanse of water, and then at the extensive bridge systems which hop from island to island. The bridges cast long shadows on the water, reminding me of how long my trek has been. I glance at the setting sun and feel a sense of ease.

The maps did not do justice to the view before me. In the distance I see the city where the assassination squad plans to kill Clive. Making my way across the bridges is going to be troublesome. I dare not conceal myself inside a truck, as the risk of detection during my exit is quite high. I notice extensive structures under many of the bridges, housing service ways, some even along both sides.

The first bridge is short and looks easy enough to cross. I simply wait for a break in traffic, then make my way to its underside. I check to see if anyone is present, and then, finding no one, sprint along the walkway to the other side. Vehicles travel overhead, oblivious to my presence. The dense vegetation alongside the road lifts my sprits even further, and as soon as the opportunity arises, I dash toward the cover.

I make it all the way to the final, and longest bridge without any difficulty. I stop and stare in wonder at the cityscape before me. Now that I am closer to my destination, I can clearly see the differences between this city, and the last one I saw; the disparity in technologies is fascinating. The city ahead is filled with gleaming skyscrapers, many of which reach far into the cloud-filled skies, far taller than anything I have observed elsewhere. Air ships fill the space between the tall buildings and seem to be the Imperium's sole means of air transport. The glinting of sunlight from what appears to be solar panels on them surprises me. Suddenly I realize that the culture before me may have never developed jet propulsion. I consider the trucks and then wonder who invented those. My best guess is not the Imperium, but instead the other factions. I am troubled as a thought comes to mind of how this faction gained such an obvious technological advantage over the other cultures in the region.

Returning my attention to the bridge before me gives me cause to pause. It is an extremely long bridge, easily the length of all the previous ones combined. It has three tall towers, one at each end, and one at the midway point. Cables sag between these towers and continue on either side to disappear inside massive buildings. Suspended below the main roadway are walkways. There are four of them, and it would appear that these are not service ways, but rather public thoroughfares.

Though the amount of road vehicles seems to have increased, I have yet to see anyone on foot. I take one more look around, and then commence the long walk.

BOOM!

The loud explosion rips though the city ahead. I stop and cringe as I hope that it was not the assassination squad eliminating Clive. I stare at thick clouds of smoke which pour from the shattered windows of one of the tall buildings. The smoke rises above it, filling the air. Remaining positive, I renew my efforts, and hurry as a variety of strange noises emanate from the city. The wailing of alarms resonates from ahead. The road vehicles headed toward the city slow down, and then stop completely. I dare to climb the metal frame and take a quick peek. I am stunned when I notice that the end of the bridge is raising up into the air, effectively cutting off all transit, including my means of crossing.

I climb back down and then continue toward the raised section. The culture may be more advanced, but the simple drawbridge elegantly cuts off all means of crossing. I arrive at the end and stare down at the shadowy waters below, attempting to determine how deep they are, and then dive in.

The second I hit the water I curve my body to reduce how far down I travel. Even so, I skim the silt at the bottom before angling back up. I hold my breath and remain below the surface as I attempt to swim toward the shore. My only swimming experience had been crossing the water way near my cave, but even so, it was enough for me to learn the basics. Eventually, I break the surface with my head, and immediately take in huge lungfuls of air. I look all around, and am astounded that, once again, no one has spotted me. I take my time getting to the shore, angling toward a group of boats which bob at the water's edge.

Now that I am closer, I stare at the source of the distant explosion and cringe; flames lick out from the upper levels of one of the damaged building. Air ships hover nearby, aiming powerful water-cannons at the shattered windows. I watch as one leaves the area, then heads toward the water, presumably to replenish its water supplies. I notice people in the distance staring up, watching the spectacle, and feel a sense of relief. The sight should prove to be an excellent distraction.

I look around as I attempt to reconcile where I am, based on what I recall from the maps in the castle. It takes me a moment; the crude two-dimensional maps displayed underground roads, and overpasses, as if everything were on the same plane. I soon realize that Clive is probably not in the building, which is on fire, but then I frown as I wonder why so many people are in these buildings. My thermal vision shows thousands of them sitting at desks, utilizing consoles. Skyscraper after skyscraper is filled with variations of the same. I decide not to bother with wondering about what they are doing, but instead focus on the residential building where Clive is purported to live. I stare at the main bridge and then almost feel the maps click as the layout of the city sinks in.

I follow the water's edge, and make my way around the island, away from the bridge. I grin widely when I see three massive buildings, all intact and connected by dozens of window filled walkways. Clive resides in one of these buildings, now to find out which one.

I study the layout intently. The interconnecting corridors occur every ten levels and stretch high into the sky. I count eleven sets in all, and nod in appreciation at the architectural skill required to accomplish the engineering feat. I notice that the upper levels of the buildings sway a little, as tall buildings do, and yet the walkways seem to remain securely in place. I focus on the upper levels, and then work my way down, scrutinizing the walkways carefully. I finally understand how they work. Each is a two-piece unit, with one side sliding inside the other, thus they are able to change in length as needed. In addition to this, where they connect to the side of the buildings is covered in a layer of flexible material. Focusing hard, I discern a series of flexible joints behind the protective covering. These multi-directional joints allow the walkways to sway as needed.

I continue to study the buildings, and the surrounding areas, as I plan how to enter one unseen. The area between the buildings is crisscrossed with walkways and gardens, some of which are quite dense. A few locals are walking about, but most are finding better vantage points to watch the burning building, and the area between these buildings affords no such view.

A low growl emanates from behind me, and steadily increases in pitch. I never heard the animal creep up on me, and slowly turn to see what creature would dare challenge me. I extend the claws in my hands as I prepare for a fight. The animal pads back and forth on four paws, its black fur bristling menacingly. Its low growls turn into barks. Its narrow head and pronounced jaw, add to the animal's fearsome appearance, and yet it wears a collar of sorts. Perhaps it is someone's pet, one that comes up to my thigh. As it turns, I notice a white tuft of fur on its chest, and even though this animal can in no way be a descendant of Madcat, that white tuft has just saved its life.

I retract my claws and crouch down. The animal's barks become less intense as it sniffs the air and approaches me apprehensively. Its ears suddenly swivel to one side, followed a split second later by its head. I also heard the faint noise, an odd popping sound, and it came from inside the nearest building.

Six people dressed in black fatigues charge out of the building, all are carrying an assortment of weapons. The men stop in the courtyard, where one of them speaks into a headset. Fortunately, I am still crouching, otherwise they may have spotted me. I tilt my head and listen intently, hoping to catch the man's words. The animal growls deeply but does not move.

"Tertiary targets eliminated, primary and secondary targets remain at large." The man reports with a hint of annoyance.

I am unable to hear the response, but the answer would be self-evident when the man states, "Understood, Sir. Strike team four out."

The man leans closer to his colleagues and venomously states, "How that fat idiot got away from us, I'll never know. He's got to be in one of these buildings. Find him and kill him."

The men intone, "Yes sir!"

The man who issued the orders shakes his head as he whispers, "Run, Clive, run. There is nothing that can save you now!"

To my surprise I find that I am stroking the animal's fur the way I used to stroke Madcat's. The creature is no longer growling, but instead is sitting with me; its tail moving back and forth, as if waiting. I stare at the creature and smile. Some animals can easily discern friend from foe, and this one seems to have decided that I am a friend.

I wait for the men to move, to see which way they go. The second they enter one of the other buildings, I run after them. The men are clearly not expecting anyone to be following them, much less to be attacked. I arrive at the doorway to see two of them running up a stairwell to the level above. Two others are entering an elevator, with the remaining two standing guard in the building's foyer. While I gather in my surroundings, the elevator doors close with a ping.

I sprint toward the two in the foyer at full speed, the excited animal bounds close behind me. Both men hesitate when they see me, their delay costs them their lives. I charge at the closer man, lower my shoulder, and drive it into his upper body as hard as I can. His chest caves in with a bone crunching sound as he is lifted off the ground. The man doubles over and collapses to the floor. Blood runs from his nose as he attempts to breathe through his shattered ribs and ruined lungs.

The second man raises his rifle, only to be stopped by my new friend. The dark furred creature bites cruelly at his arm and hangs on as the man attempts to shake the animal off. I rake my extended claws across the man's face, ripping his skin to the bone. He screams in agony and drops his weapon. He lifts his hands to his flailed skin, just as I slam my elbow into his nose. The bone snaps under the force of the impact, driving fragments into his brain. He collapses to the ground, his body twitches and spasms, as his brain shuts down. The animal senses victory and finally lets go of the man's arm.

Pop… Pop… Pop…

The muffled gunfire alerts me to the men returning from upstairs. Their shots are panicky and wild, and all miss me, though not by much. I dive and roll toward the steps as more shots scuff the floor and walls around me. Something tugs at my left shoulder as I lunge at the men. I land between them, and slash at their stomachs. To my surprise my claws leave deep grooves in the material they wear, but do not penetrate. I lift both hands ramming my claws under their chins and into their throats, then rip them out. Blood sprays and splatters in all directions, splashing the animal which still follows me. The bodies begin to tumble grotesquely down the steps, smearing even more blood as they go.

I quickly turn my attention to the bank of elevators. The one containing the armed men is still on the move, or at least that is what the increasing numbers above the entry to it indicate. The bodies topple to the ground level as I bound up the stairwell, my blood covered companion once more, close behind.

I glance at my left shoulder and am surprised to see three holes. Blood seeps from the wounds indicating that the projectiles have penetrated my scales, but not deeply enough to cause any serious injury. Clearly weapons technology is improving on this planet.

I arrive at the next level and am surprised to see people panicking in all directions. A female runs my way, screaming. Her eyes widen when she notices me. Her screams turn shrill as she falls to the ground and slides into my legs. A stain spreads from between her legs while the smell of urine assaults my nose. She flops about as if injured, but I can see nothing that would cause her to act this way.

Ignoring her, and the other panicking people, I watch the bank of elevators, and in particular the one which contains the armed men. The number above the elevator stops, hopefully indicting the level at which the armed assailants have exited.

I glance around and see a curved metal staircase extending to the tall ceiling, and beyond. Clearly, it is only to be used in emergency situations, as I cannot imagine anyone climbing the vast number of steps it must contain.

The rattle of weapons fire from the level below is immediately followed by the shrill echoes of people screaming. I glance at the animal next to me, then sprint for the metal staircase. The creature races ahead of me, and then bounds up the spiral metal staircase, leaving bloody paw prints in its wake. Why some animals like me is baffling but pleasing none-the-less. I rush after the animal, taking the steps three at a time. My exertions bend and buckle the steps with each leap. They creak alarmingly, but do not break. My eager companion leads the way, puffing and panting as the stairwell continues upward. While the main level was open, those above are sealed off by doorways, each one numbered, indicating the level.

The steps are wide enough that I overtake the tiring animal. At level fifty-eight I am unexpectedly confronted by a fat man in a suit. I stop and stare at his quivering hands, and the pair of guns they hold. He shakily aims them at the snarling animal which has caught up to me. Before the overweight man can decide to shoot, I lunge at him.

I slap the weapons from his hands as I question, "Clive?"

The man's eyes open wider, while his mouth drops open. He nods, clearly terrified, but does not speak.

"I am not here to kill you; I am here to help you." I utter bluntly.

The man's face twitches as he stares at me, his bulging eyes fill with tears as fear overcomes him. He moans as he urinates in his pants and collapses. I catch him before he falls down the stairwell.

I stare at the pathetic man and sigh as I mutter, "Natalie, I am glad you are not here to witness your pitiful descendant."

Voices rise from below, cutting off my thoughts. The words are incoherent, but their tone is unmistakable.

I shake the man and say, "Run you fool, an assassination squad is on its way, and unlike me, they do want to kill you."

Clive's jaw drops in surprise, but that is all he does. He still stands before me, unmoving.

I shove him as I state, "I knew Natalie, and I promised her that I would protect her and her kin."

"Natalie?" Clive states in confusion as he staggers backward.

Clive's brow creases, and then suddenly it dawns on him who I am referring to. His mouth opens and closes silently as his mind tries to rationalize what that means. He finally turns, opens the door to the level we are on, and runs. His short stubby legs struggle to carry his chubby body any quicker than a fast walk. I stare at the fleeing man in antipathy. This is the linage that I am protecting! I shake my head as I recall the memories of Natalie and Madcat, and their bravery.

The animal sits at my side and tilts its head, as if it does not understand why we let the man go, especially after we chased him down. I pat the animal's head and state, "I know!"

Bullets zing past me as gunfire rattles from below. I duck through the doorway Clive ran through, and then follow the noise of his passage. His heavy footfalls discernible, even on the carpet flooring. I hurry after the sound, and soon come across another stairway, one with high sides to prevent people from falling to the level below. I follow the steps downward, and easily catch up to Clive. Surprisingly the animal stays with me, keeping pace, and even seems to be relishing in the thrill of the chase.

We rush down a few levels, and then I notice one of the passageways which extends between the buildings. I grab Clive's sweaty shoulder, and then roughly direct him down it. His chest heaves from his hard breathing, while sweat drips from his forehead. He stares at the long corridor, then hesitantly complies.

I hurry back to the stairway, hide out of sight beside it, and wait. The animal stares at Clive, then back at me, and then decides to join me. I do not have to wait long. The animal's ears twitch at the sound of running footfalls. Four or five people are running down the steps, but I am unable to determine if they belong to the assailants.

The first of them reaches the bottom and stops. The man, who is armed with a large weapon, turns as he looks around. He notices Clive, before turning all the way, and thus does not see me crouched down behind him. He lifts his rifle and takes careful aim at Clive.

Before he can fire, I lunge at him, slashing at his back with my extended claws. He cries out in pain as I rip his back wide open, exposing his spine. The weapon falls from his lifeless fingers when I rip my claws out, severing his spinal cord. As the dying man collapses to the ground, I turn to the steps, and come face to face with four more armed men. Their brief hesitation is their undoing.

I immediately charge the group, slashing wildly as I get to them. I put all my force into driving my claws through their body armor and succeed. The first man staggers before me, blinking in surprise as his intestines spill onto the floor at his feet. He drops his weapon and attempts to hold the rest of his insides in, but it is too late for him. Even as he falls to the ground, the second of the group joins him, his throat slashed through to the bone, almost cleaving his head from his body. A bloody fountain sprays the area, spurting in all directions as the man spins around before falling to the steps, where he slides to the bottom. The animal joins in just in time to be grotesquely sprayed once more with blood.

The last two men hurriedly swing their rifles up. I dive between them, violently ripping the weapons from their hands, and then smash their heads with them. The weapons shatter against their heads, knocking them to the ground. I stomp, caving their skulls in, slopping their brains all over the carpet, adding to the bloody mix.

Glancing up, I see another man standing at the top of the steps. He does not carry any weapons, but instead stands with his shaking hands outstretched, as if to ward off the sight before him. I notice an expanding wet patch on the front of his pants and shake my head. Does everyone have to urinate themselves when they see me?

The man flinches as the sound of gunfire fills the air. He suddenly staggers, his back arches and his arms flail out. I frown at the expanding blossoms of blood on his body. The gunfire continues unabated, turning his chest into an explosive mess of exit wounds as projectiles rip through his body. The force of the impacts drives him forward, and down the steps toward me.

Before his bullet riddled body hits the ground, I turn and flee. I sprint after Clive, my footfalls shaking the passageway as I easily catch up to the plodding man. His sweat covered shirt heaves up and down with each labored and wheezing breath. I glance ahead and see that we are less than halfway along the corridor, and his pace is slowing. His fitness level is pathetic and disgusts me. The animal bounds ahead, clearly enjoying the race. I grab Clive's arm and propel him forward as fast as I can. He stumbles, but my grip prevents him from falling.

With stark realization I see that we will not make it to the end in time and, more importantly, I doubt that my scales will provide enough protection against the projectiles of this era. I glance out one of the windows as I run past and get a crazy notion.

I shove Clive ahead and then stop. He trips and almost falls, but he truly surprises me when he does not. The man actually moves a little faster, clearly understanding that his very life depends on it.

I look out the window and quickly scrutinize the corridors below me. As suspected, they are two-piece units, hinged on each end. I return to the midpoint of the corridor I am in, and easily see where the two sections slide in and out of each other. I begin tearing the walls apart, exposing the framework, and then rip out a guide rail. I jump up and down as hard as I can on the section we came from, and where I expect the gun toting assailants to appear any second. The entire passageway suddenly lurches downward a short distance, then stops at it catches. I tear at the roof panels and then the floor panels, exposing more guide rails, which I recklessly rip out.

Without warning, the floor lurches downward, giving the corridor a banana-like appearance as it sags in the middle. Wind begins to howl through the openings, causing both sections to shake and shudder. I slam all my body weight into the floor causing the floor to shudder as the joints on the side of the building are strained beyond their design tolerance. Unexpectedly, my foot smashes through and dangles in the air. The remaining metal framework creaks and groans as I removed it.

Projectiles strike the walls all around me. I look up the sloping corridor, and straight at a dozen heavily armed men. I watch helplessly as three of them take aim at me with long barreled weapons.

The entire floor suddenly lurches downward, and then gives way completely.

I twist and leap for the side Clive is still running down. I catch the lip of the dangling walkway with my claws, and then remain still as the hinges on the distant wall flex and buckle, yet miraculously hold. I take precious seconds securing my grip before I cautiously climb into the corridor. I turn back and see the other side hanging uselessly against the building, blocking my view of the gunmen. I grin as I realize that the collapsed section is not as useless as I first thought; the gunmen cannot see me to fire their weapons.

I make my way up the sloping floor as fast as I can, while attempting to avoid straining the hinges. Clive is almost to the end when he trips and stumbles. Events appear to slow down as he falls forward, his arms outstretched. Realizing what is about to happen, I sprint. My heels dig deep grooves as I put all my efforts into getting to the end. Clive hits the ground hard, shaking the floor and knocking the wind out of himself with a huge swoosh. The floor lurches as one of the upper hinges tears away from the building. The others are not far from failing.

My animal companion has made it all the way to the end, and now sits, watching us. The creature tilts its head, as if out of curiosity, as Clive begins to slide down the sloping floor toward me. I dig my claws in the floor as it shudders and shakes, the remaining hinges creaking alarmingly. I catch his sliding body with my left arm as the remaining upper hinge fails. The walkway freefalls toward the building, and slams into it, shattering glass in all directions.

Dangling against what was the floor, I glance down at the roof of the corridor far below, and then look upward to the lip of the walkway. It is closer than I had first thought, but it may as well not be. My view of the ground is limited to what I can see through the twisted opening of the corridor.

Clive's ear-piercing scream fills the air when he glances downward. He kicks his feet in panic, almost breaking free of my grip.

I snarl into his ear, "Are you dim witted? If I let go of you, you will fall. Remain still if you wish to live."

He stops wriggling, and instead hyperventilates as fear overcomes him. I glance up once more, and then stop and look straight ahead through a hole in the floor. A shattered window, beyond which is an empty room, greets my eyes. I wonder how I am going to cut my way through while holding Clive in one arm.

"Clive," I state firmly, "In my pouch is a device. You must reach in and get it."

The man blinks at me fearfully, but slowly complies. I spend an agonizing amount of time instructing the bumbling man on how to turn it on and operate it. I hold my breath as he almost drops the tool, then relax as he finally begins to carve into the floor before us.

Small pieces fall away and crash onto the roof of the corridor below us. A larger piece breaks free and tumbles all the way to the ground, where curious onlookers gaze upward. I watch as the people below flee. My face flinches when I see a group of armed men appear in my restricted view and aim their weapons up at me.

"Clive, hurry!" I state unnecessarily as projectiles ping the walls around us.

I am surprised when instead of freezing up, Clive speeds up, cutting away larger and larger pieces, until there is enough room for him to squeeze through.

"That's enough," I state, adding, "now, put my tool away."

Clive stares at me with wide eyes as he puts it away and asks, "How do we get through."

Without warning I twist and hurl him through the opening. Clive lands on the floor, and rolls to a stop. A projectile strikes my leg, digging a furrow along my scales, before it skims past my head, narrowly missing my face. I dive through the opening, smashing my way through, and land where Clive was. Fortunately, he had the presence of mind to scurry away.

A loud tearing noise from outside draws my attention. I watch as the battered walkway breaks free and falls. It crashes into the one below, and smashes through it to impact onto the one beneath it, where it clips the edge and then cartwheels all the way to the ground. The assailants on the ground scatter as debris rains down all around them.

I glance upward to see the animal looking down at me. It vanishes from sight as the sound of gunfire emanates from the building opposite me. I dive to the ground, shoving Clive down as projectiles ping into the walls all around us.

"Follow me!" I instruct, as I crawl toward an open door.

Clive wriggles on his bulging belly as he does his best to follow me. I make my way through the door, and into an open area. A wide stairway leads in both directions, while a bank of elevators is clearly in view. I frown as I see the numbers above two of the elevators increasing, indicating that they are coming up from below.

I grab Clive and shove him toward a stairwell. Unexpectedly, we come face to face with a gun wielding man. His combat attire matches that of the men we are avoiding. He lifts his weapon up fast, but I am quicker. With a single swipe, I slice his shoulder to the bone, snapping the tendons which run down his arm.

The man screams in agony as his useless arm drops the weapon. I shove his head hard, pushing him backward down the stairs into three more similarly garbed men. The falling man collides with them in a tangle of arms and legs, effectively slowing them down. I turn to find that Clive is already making his way upstairs as fast as his legs will carry him. I glance across at the elevators and suddenly realize what they are planning.

"Keep running!" I shout at Clive as I follow him.

We run up one level then, with my help, another, before Clive is spent. Arriving at the level with the corridor, I hear the distinctive dinging sound of the elevators arriving. I stare at the animal, which is waiting for us, and then shield Clive from a hail of projectiles which spew forth from across the way.

I roar in pain as three find their mark in my right shoulder. I feel them thud into my scales, and then rip through them, only to be stopped by my shoulder blade. I continue and manage to get to the next level where I examine Clive for any sign of injury. Finding none, I turn to the animal, and see it sitting, wagging its long tail.

A burst of weapons' fire reaches my ears, followed by another. The chorus of fire increases to that of a full firefight. I wonder who is shooting at who and dare to sneak down and look.

Dozens of men lay dead on the steps, more near the elevators. A second group of men seem to be responsible, these are also dressed in dark garb, and heavily armed. One of them notices me and does the most unexpected thing.

The man drops his weapon and lifts his empty hands while he loudly states, "We will not harm you, Mamluk."

My brows crease as I shout back, "You know my name! How?"

"Natalie wrote many things about you, so that should you ever appear in our midst we would understand that you are not our enemy." The man replies as he indicates for his colleagues to lower their weapons.

"If you are truly my friend, then why is Madcat's pelt hanging like some trophy?" I spit.

The man shakes his head as he replies, "I don't know our history properly, but I can attest that your pet died a natural death at Natalie's feet, guarding her to the end."

A short woman, dressed in civilian clothes, steps into view. She gulps, and then hesitantly speaks. "I am Premier Peltar, and I offer you my word that we are here to assist you." She glances at the soldiers warily, then steps closer.

Clive runs down the steps past me and falls to his knees. Tears stream down his face as he says, "Premier, I thank you for coming to my aid."

The woman stares at Clive and questions, "Who are you?"

I begin to chuckle as I stride downstairs. The animal follows, and then sits next to me when I stop. I watch the soldiers for any sign of hostility, but see none, and although I outwardly relax, I remain vigilant.

I nod to Clive and state, "He is of Natalie's bloodline. That why the others were trying to kill him."

Premier Peltar relaxes as she replies, "I had no idea he was a descendant, and doubt that anyone would know that. But he is an outspoken politician and a reformist, which does not bode well with certain groups."

I stare at Clive in confusion as I continue, "But his name was on a plaque, at the old castle where the statue is of Natalie."

The woman shakes her head and shrugs her shoulders, "Perhaps the historians can shed some light on the matter."

She turns to the soldiers and instructs, "Seal the building, and secure safe passage for us."

The soldiers turn to leave when a young boy unexpectedly runs out from a doorway. Two of the men instantly lift their weapons and take aim. I snarl aggressively as I back toward the steps. The boy runs my way, with weapons aimed at his back. The child is oblivious to the danger he is in as he runs toward me, his eyes affixed solidly on the animal at my side. The boy suddenly notices me; he opens his eyes wide as he falls to the ground and moans fearfully as he attempts to scramble backward.

The animal at my side bounds toward the boy, its tail wagging, clearly enjoying the game. The soldiers lower their weapons, while Premier Peltar lets go of the breath she was holding.

To my surprise I realize that Clive has stepped in front me, with his arms outstretched, as if to shield me from the soldiers.

I put my hand on his shoulder and state, "Natalie would be proud, Clive."

The man turns to me, and with a shaky voice says, "I have to admit, I was scared they would shoot anyway."

"Only a fool ignores their fears, just do not let them dictate your actions." I reply.

One of the soldiers walks up to the Premier and whispers quietly, "The forces are still sweeping the building, but we have cleared a path to the roof."

Remaining emotionless, I let my gaze wander over my surroundings, as my keen sense of hearing picks up every word.

Premier Peltar directs her attention my way and says, "The guard has secured the path to the roof."

The guard!

I instantly tense up. Could it be the same guard that ousted Jerry? I glance around warily, but do not notice anything out of the ordinary. With alarm, I realize that there are now twenty soldiers standing at strategic points, essentially containing me in a protective perimeter, or are they ready to annihilate me?

I notice Clive staring at me strangely, then as if sensing my tension, he states loudly. "Premier Peltar, would you please accompany me with my friend as we make our way to the roof. This being is as intelligent as he is tough and could perhaps offer us more technology." Clive glances at me and makes a strange gesture with his face.

Premier Peltar does not hesitate and replies, "It would be an honor to listen to Mamluk."

She turns to me as she adds, "Many of us felt that you were a myth; that Natalie made you up."

I tilt my head as I state, "You seem well versed in Natalie's history, and yet did not know that Clive was a descendant. Why is that?"

Premier Peltar hesitates before answering, and then finally admits, "I had to be briefed on our early history when reports of a strange creature marauding through the city streets came to my desk. I had already ordered forces to contend with the terror group, but it was not until moments ago that we realized you were battling them too."

Clive tentatively raises a hand as he requests, "Premier, may I?"

"Of course." She replies diplomatically.

Clive takes a deep breath and then begins, "All children are taught that Natalie led our early settlers to this island chain, while her alien friend sacrificed himself against the forces that were seeking her out."

He takes a deep breath, then glances at Premier Peltar before continuing, "Once the island chain was secured, Natalie led a small force back to the villa, where she found the burned body of her husband, and buried him. Her force returned with many strange artifacts which she dedicated her life attempting to solve."

Premier Peltar proudly interjects, "Her earliest solar panels are on display, and are so advanced that our scientists are still unsure how they work. They did steer our technology in the right direction though, allowing us to have an abundance of energy."

I roll my aching shoulder and cringe as one of the projectiles rubs against the bone. Ignoring the discomfort, I ask curiously, "When you say artifacts. What else did she bring back?"

Clive answers excitedly, "Oh, I know this one. She brought back wires, and parts of what would eventually be a steam powered generator, and a strange contraption we have yet to figure out. The only thing she was missing was a way of storing the energy, and it was not until many years later we realized that her team must have missed a component."

I nod as I reply, "It was not left behind, it was a storage power cell, and I took it. I would like to see the artifacts you found."

Premier Peltar hesitates, and then points to one of her guards and instructs, "Tell the archivists to release them into my care."

The man stares blankly for a moment, then nods, and briskly walks toward the elevators.

The Premier calls after the man, further instructing, "Have the artifacts delivered to the Main Assembly Chambers."

The man stops, turns, then replies respectfully, "Yes, Premier."

I watch the man continue on his way, then warily plod alongside Premier Peltar and Clive as they walk toward the Elevators. The guards keep their weapons pointed outward, as they keep a watchful eye. The elevator creaks and groans in protest as I step inside, causing the others to glance at me nervously. I consider the floor, and the metal steps from earlier and frown. I am not that heavy therefore it seems that these people do not build a lot of redundancy into their designs. To be on the safe side I keep my rear claws retracted. I have no desire to rip the floor open. The elevator moves upward and shakes and shudders as we are swiftly transported to the roof.

It is dark outside, but not pitch black. The city's lights create a dull glow in the night sky, reducing the number of stars that I can see. The feeble lights on the rooftop do little more than create gloomy shadows outside their radius. I easily identify the five guards standing by the gondola of one of their airships. The massive craft is moored by long ropes to anchor points on each side, its bulbous upper workings pull on the ropes as it attempts to drift away in the subtle breeze. Other city buildings also have a smattering of lights, some with airships moored to their rooftops as well.

While I have no trouble seeing in the dim lighting, Clive and the Premier struggle to adjust, and have to be led. I stare intently at the flooring of the gondola, and seconds later find what I am looking for. I stride inside, keeping my weight on the flush rivet heads, which indicate where the main supports run underneath. The area inside is more spacious than I first thought, and easily accommodates everyone, including the guards, and the pilot.

"Weapons keeping!" Barks one of the soldiers loudly.

The soldiers glance apprehensively in my direction, then stow their weapons as ordered. I am not concerned with their glances at myself, or each other. Their fear is so great; it is almost a tangible thing. Occasional mumbles reach my ears, as the soldiers talk quietly amongst themselves.

I watch with fascination as the ropes retract, seemingly automatically. We lift into the sky with only the slightest whir of distant propeller blades to indicate our means of propulsion. I glance upward with mild concern as I recall that this is a solar powered craft. Taking care to place my feet on the main supports, I make my way to the pilot station.

The soldier who seems to be the one in charge quiets his men when he says, "We are Premier Peltar's personal guard, and should be honored to be accompanying this alien to the Assembly, not frightened." The man turns to me, stiffens up, and then stands at rigid attention.

I glance at the men as I comment, "I am Mamluk. If you do me no I harm, then you shall all live."

Before anyone can reply, I step next to the pilot and ask, "Where is the power reserve indicator?"

The pilot gulps, then as a bead of sweat works its way down the side of his face he points to his console. I frown as I stare at a half circle with a needle hovering at the mid-way mark. The needle slowly drifts to the left as we move through the air. I stare ahead through a series of small windows at the cityscape before me. We are descending slowly between two colossal skyscrapers and seem to be travelling along a purpose-built air corridor.

We move away from the main island, and slowly continue our descent toward a smaller, well-lit land mass. I gauge our rate of progress to that of the needle, and then notice that the pilot is sweating profusely, confirming my own suspicions. These craft are not usually used at night. Glancing back at the others, it is clear they are oblivious to our plight.

Turning to the pilot I quietly ask, "Will this craft make it?"

The pilot shrugs his shoulders, and then says, "It will be close."

"Turn off all the lights." I instruct, as if the obvious answer is to reduce the power drain.

The pilot turns and looks at the Premier, then shakes his head fearfully.

"How is it that this craft has such a limited range?" I question.

The man picks his head up and states with pride, "I kept all systems running, in preparation for an immediate launch, as per protocol."

I stride away from the obstinate man. He would rather risk running out of power than admit the craft's limitations to the Premier. However, I am not concerned. If the craft runs out of power, we will simply drift with the wind, or land sooner than expected.

As I sit back down one of the soldiers approaches me and says, "I see that you were injured."

I stare at the man intently as I reply, "Yes, I was struck by the projectiles your weapons use."

"I am only a field medic, but I can look if you like." The man continues.

I stare into his eyes, evaluating his demeanor, then twist around as I reply, "You may attempt to remove them."

The man walks to a panel inside, opens it and removes a large box. He takes out a pair of forceps, some bandaging material, and a tube which contains an unknown substance. The others watch, fascinated.

He walks back to me and says, "This may hurt."

I turn my head and lock eyes with him as I respond, "I am sure it will."

I relax my scales in an attempt to make his task easier. However, the second he inserts the tip of the forceps, they involuntarily harden. I grunt as he digs into my shoulder. He removes the projectiles, one by one, dropping each into a small container. Once he is done, he squeezes the tube, squirting its contents into the holes. I feel a strange mild numbing sensation as he applies bandages to the wounds.

I roll my shoulder, then turn to the man and say approvingly, "Great work. You have my gratitude."

The soldier smiles warmly, nods, and replies, "The honor is mine, Mister Mamluk."

I turn and watch with interest as the pilot becomes more apprehensive. A few moments later the lights dim. The guards become restless; it is clear they understand what is going on. Premier Peltar glances at the dim lights, as if confused, then continues her discussion with Clive. As the time passes, the pilot visibly relaxes.

Celebration

The craft lands with a noticeable bump, which, though it jostles everyone, no one seems concerned. The soldiers immediately disembark and grab the ropes as they snake out from their external storage spaces. Once the craft is secured, the Premier steps out. I stride outside and am surprised by our location. We are resting on a vast area filled with solar panels. Dozens of airships occupy other mooring stations. Each is tethered by a series of ropes, with additional cables snaking out from ground panels, connecting to the rear of the gondolas. Off in the distance is a series of well-lit buildings. Unlike the tall cityscape we just left, these buildings are only three to four levels in height and seem to sprawl across the landscape.

None of the soldiers seem to be paying me any attention, and if anything, seem more relaxed now that we are on the ground. The man who oversaw them marches to me, stops briskly, then says, "It is an honor to have met you, Mister Mamluk." The man salutes, then walks away, issuing orders to his men as he returns to his duties.

Clive swings his head around skittishly; he is clearly more nervous than me. He waves in my direction, to get my attention, and says, "I have never been here. This island is off limits to all, except the Assembly members and their families."

Premier Peltar walks to me and, as she waves around with her arms, states with pride, "Welcome to Assembly Island." She smiles and bows slightly.

I gaze around, slightly confused. The mere sight of me makes most of the locals either wet themselves, or flee, and yet the people here seem unperturbed by my visage.

The Premier motions ahead and says, "Please walk with me to the Assembly Chambers"

I follow the Premier with mounting curiosity. Clive continues to gape as he tags along. We walk a short distance, then step up onto a sled. The sled's electric motors are almost silent as they propel us along. The lights along the path are evenly spaced and cast no shadows onto the manicured gardens which line both sides.

Premier Peltar turns to me and says, "I think you will be pleasantly surprised by what you find."

She turns to Clive, and with a dead serious tone informs him, "And Clive. If you enter the Assembly Chamber, you may never leave the island again. What you are about to witness is a closely guarded secret."

Clive glances around thoughtfully, then says, "Well, it's not as if it's that safe for me back there anyway!"

We ride in silence for a few moments, before the sled stops outside a large four-story building. The Premier leads us inside, where we walk along a carpeted corridor until we arrive at massive double doors.

The Premier opens the doors as she announces energetically, "Welcome to the Main Assembly."

I stride inside the bright room, then stop and stare at the unexpected spectacle. Hundreds of people stand and begin clapping. I glance around looking for threats, and seeing none, relax and take in the chamber.

The area is rounded, with at least three hundred seats arrayed in rising tiers in a full circle around a central area where a small platform rests. In the midst of this platform I see a metallic pole with an odd-looking object resting on its top. Gazing around I see that the entire room is filled with people; virtually every seat has a person standing before it.

The Premier walks toward the platform and, once there, speaks into the object. Her voice echoes powerfully around the chamber, clearly amplified. "Thank you for joining me at this late hour, but as you can see, we have an unprecedented event taking place, one that proves that the historians were telling the truth."

The Premier beckons me over as she continues, "Tonight, I present to you the alien, Mamluk. This is the being who saved our founders, and thanks to his gifts, allowed us to advance technologically, and thereby, to thrive. We owe Mamluk everything!"

The hall reverberates in cheering and hearty clapping as I make my way to the central area.

The Premier leans close to me and whispers, "If you have any words, we would be honored to hear them."

I stand before the microphone, and, while the noise diminishes, gather my thoughts. I gaze around the chamber as the people sit, and then speak, "I have been hunted and persecuted, by the people of this world for many years. Standing here, being respected, is an honor. You have earned my gratitude, something I do not give lightly."

A small commotion nearby gets my attention. A group of people approaches, all carrying large boxes. They place these at my feet, and then open them. I immediately recognize the makeshift charger for my crafting tool, a few sections of wiring, and fragments of solar panels. Surprisingly as more boxes are opened, a couple of them contain complete solar panels. Other boxes contain the remnants of the boiler system which I had built in the basement of the villa.

After a few moments of reflecting on the past, I turn back to the crowd and state, "Natalie would be proud of what you have accomplished here, but she may not be so proud of you destroying a city filled with non-combatants."

The Premier lowers her head and then solemnly says, "The decision to use the weapon was a difficult one. The conflict between the two factions had been waging for years and had taken the lives of hundreds of thousands of young men and women on both sides. They were also consuming vast amounts of resources, to the point of failing to feed their own people. We felt that we had to act and put an end to the war once and for all."

As I listen, I take in the room in greater detail, I notice a series of images lining the walls. Many of these depict Natalie or Madcat, but a few of them are amazingly accurate drawings of me. Some are of me using my crafting tool, others are of me gazing into the distance. It suddenly dawns on me that these appear to have been drawn while I was actually performing these tasks.

"I understand." I reply.

Before she can respond I point to the pictures and ask, "Those drawings of me. Were they done by Natalie?"

"The historians believe so!" She replies excitedly.

"I did not know that she could draw." I state slowly as I reflect on the villa.

The Premier turns to me in awe, "I'm still having trouble comprehending that you are the same being who lived during the time of our founders."

I smile and, speaking in a soft tone, narrate, "I recall a time when Natalie was a young girl. She would hold onto Madcat's fur and get dragged around the villa." My tone turns serious as I continue, "I also recall the betrayal by Jerry's son. Something I vowed to correct by eliminating his bloodline."

An unsteady murmuring fills the chamber as the meaning behind my words sinks in. Some of those present shift uncomfortably in their seats.

Premier Peltar lifts her hand and waits until the noise subsides. She turns to me and asks, "You would punish those, whose only crime is being the descendant of a man who wronged you?"

"His linage deserves to end." I state bluntly.

The Premier frowns as she states emphatically, "But these descendants are innocent. They have not done anything to you. How can you hold those people accountable for actions they did not take, and perhaps never would?"

"I deserve my vengeance!" I retort.

"Do you?" She questions boldly as she lifts her steely gaze to meet mine.

I stare intently at the diminutive woman, and am about to respond, when it dawns on me that if I carry out my promise, I would be no better than Jerry's son. I then consider what Natalie would have done.

After a moment of reflecting, I reply, "Perhaps too much time has passed."

She nods as she says, "The man who betrayed you did not live long. He was killed by his guards. If the story goes correctly, it was something to do with the guards being questioned about your demise. You see, history has it that you were killed."

I feel a strange clarity as I respond, "That would explain why no one found me, no one was looking."

She shrugs her shoulders as she replies, "There were a few who did not believe that you were dead, but not many. It was well known that you were grievously injured."

"I was seriously injured, yes." I admit.

"Well," She continues, "your body was never recovered, leaving doubts as to your death. But then as the years passed, and you did not resurface, it was assumed that you crawled off to die in some isolated place."

I gaze at those assembled and decide that I like these people. I consider my promise to Natalie, and then make my decision. I hold my crafting tool aloft and state, "I will reveal to you a method of storing power!"

The crowd roars approvingly, then as I lift my hand, they begin to quiet back down.

I glance at Clive, and then add, "I will also show you how to clean up radiation, such as from the city that was devastated."

The assembly turns to chaos as people cheer, clap, and whistle, signifying their approval. I lift my arm, to quiet the crowd once more, but instead the noise level increases. The bedlam is deafening, even to me.

Premier Peltar is also unable to subdue the crowd, so instead she leans close to me and shouts, "We may as well leave!"

The next few days are a complete whirlwind of activity. I am assigned spacious quarters, and a large facility with a team of experts. Clive is assigned to me as my intermediary, thus avoiding my need for direct contact with the teams of people, unless absolutely necessary. He seems to relish in his new responsibilities and takes them on with gusto. Everyone works with me around the clock as I freely share my knowledge. Premier Peltar's instructions that I be given unlimited resources to work with, speeds up the process, and has many benefits.

The days come and go as I take advantage of their generosity and build a new charger for my construction tool. I also construct a couple of power storage units, and then charge them using the city's power grid. These units are larger than the one in the shuttle yet store less power. The infrastructure needed for their mass production will take considerable time and effort, but I am sure that they will succeed. I take one of these units and secure it in a crate. I am reminded of my time at the villa, and rather than becoming comfortable and complacent, I work as fast as I can.

The construction of radiation cleanup tools takes the longest time. Eventually I am convinced that the people assigned to the task, comprehend not only how to use the tools, but how to manufacture more. I also learn that the weapon used, was discovered by accident. These people were experimenting with various elements in their quest to find a way of storing electricity, and in doing so, found an element that, when an electrical charge is applied, results in a massive fission-like detonation.

I examine their solar panels, and then advise of ways to improve them. The teams whine that my plan will require them to build completely new facilities, but the second I demonstrate the improvements in power collection, all grumblings cease. In fact, this team is the first to make a working prototype. I grin as I listen to Clive raving about the successful test of a new solar cell.

I wake one morning and realize that I have honored my obligations to Natalie, and am now free to return to my craft, and to hopefully leave this planet once and for all. I spend the day packing a dozen solar panels, a second power storage unit, and a huge sheet of metal, which I plan to use to secure the window.

Premier Peltar hurries into my quarters. Before I can comment, she questions, "You're leaving already? It's only been a matter of months; we still have so much more to do."

I turn to her and reply, "I have done all I said I would do, it is time I return to my kind."

She opens her mouth to speak, and then changes her mind. After a few moments of silence, she says, "I will secure an airship for your goods."

Clive enters the room, huffing and puffing as usual, his shirt drenched in sweat. Although he is fitter than when I first met him, he still has a long way to go. The man wheezes, "See, I told you he was going!"

I turn to him and say, "Clive, you have exceeded my expectations!"

"Will I ever see you again?" He asks with a pained expression as he glances back and forth from the Premier to me.

"I doubt it" I reply candidly as I continue to pack my belongings. I have accumulated more than I thought I had.

The Premier stares at me and says, "You are a strange being; a cold-blooded killer, and yet here you are helping us."

I stop what I am doing and stare at the two people. "Few beings have earned my gratitude. Madcat was the first, then Natalie, and now Clive."

The Premier frowns as she asks, "What of Jerry?"

"He and I had an agreement, nothing more." I reply bluntly.

She nods, and then says, "I will arrange for that airship and crew."

I watch her leave and then address Clive. "Would you like to accompany me to the city limits?"

"Me?" Clive exclaims, shocked at my request. "Yes!" He quickly stammers, "Yes!"

By the time I have finished packing I have three crates; one for each of the two storage units, while the third is filled with solar panels. The sheet of metal is too large to fit in a crate, and rests alongside them instead.

I watch as crews ferry the crates outside, and then once I confirm that I have everything, I leave my quarters. I stride down the hallway and stop as I step outside. The Assembly members line both sides of the walkway for as far as I can see, and by the looks of things, all three hundred are present.

Premier Peltar and Clive stand before me on a transport sled, silently waiting. I step onto the sled then, as we move out, the people who line the sides begin clapping. I stare in wonder at the spectacle. These people gaze at me with reverence and respect. Usually, the mere sight of me causes most people who see me, to flee, or react in fear.

The three of us travel to a massive airship. The sunlight glints and gleams off its solar panels. The amount of light reflecting off them tells me that these are the original panels, the newer technology

I shared absorbs much more light, thus they do not reflect as much. Beneath the airship is a large gondola, next to which I see the same pilot and guardsmen I flew to the island with.

The Premier turns to me and says, "These people are loyal and can be trusted. No one will disclose where they take you."

I turn to the gathering and then seeing their expectant faces, offer a few words, "May you thrive in peace. Who knows, perhaps one day we shall meet amongst the stars?"

As I turn and stride onto the airship it dawns on me that I do not know how the Protectorate incorporates worlds like these into their fold. Perhaps they wait for a certain technology level? I muse. Clive follows me onboard, and then sits with the soldiers.

The pilot of the airship waves and smiles at me as he asks, "Where do you want me to take you?"

I make sure I place my feet on the rivet heads as I make my way to his side. I frown as we gain altitude, and then notice a distant volcano. I point to it and say, "Make for the lava flows." I still like the idea that most think I live near the lava fields.

"Yes, Sir!" He replies excitedly.

We gain speed and altitude, until finally the city is far behind us. A few clouds drift in the light wind across the sky, giving me an idea. I lean close to the pilot and, while pointing ahead, quietly tell him, "Descend into those clouds, and then slowly turn toward the city that was bombed."

The pilot obliges immediately, and wordlessly. The descent and turn are barely perceptible, such is his skill. I notice sweat beads forming on his forehead and ask, "What is the problem?"

He glances at me nervously as he replies, "I have never been here, and am unsure how high the mountains are."

I glance at his controls and ask, "You do not have an altimeter?"

"A what?" he replies, answering my question for me.

"Oh my!" I reply, "So you just guess your altitude?" I state, more than inquire.

"Ah huh." He says.

We drift below the clouds and. to our relief, discover that we are safe. Something catches my attention; I turn my head sharply to the left to see. There, alongside us, seemingly coming out of the clouds, is a cliff face. Sweat rolls down the pilot's face as he attempts to arrest our descent, while at the same time works to swing us away from the wall of rocks.

I glance to the right, and then tap the pilot on the shoulder and point. I stare at the cliffs on either side of us, and then as we begin to climb, instruct, "No! Keep us in this valley for as long as you can."

The pilot's face twitches as he adjusts our course and heading to follow the ravine's curves. I watch with fascination as the man's skills are put to the test. This is an airship after all, and it clearly responds sluggishly to his input. He slows our forward momentum as the valley narrows, but he still threads the massive airship through the winding ravine with precision. Even with the sun high overhead, we are so deep in the canyon that we spend much of the time in the shadows of the cliff walls.

We exit the ravine to a welcoming sight. The roadway to the villa is in the next valley, and nearby. The pilot keeps our altitude low as we skim over the scorched grasslands, and then the lava. I glance to where my cave is, but do not draw any attention to it. The entrance appears to be undisturbed.

As the devastated city comes into view, I instruct the pilot, "It is not safe for you to venture any closer. Land the craft in the field near that burned forest, and I shall proceed the rest of the way on foot."

"You live near the city?" Clive asks with obvious awe. "No wonder you don't want us to use energy bombs anymore!"

"I live on the far side of the city," I lie, "but I wish to obtain Madcat's pelt, and give it the respect it deserves."

The pilot lowers the craft until the gondola is resting on the singed grass. The soldiers quickly unload the crates, and then re-board the craft, keen to be away from the obvious danger of the lava, and the invisible threat of radiation poisoning. Clive hangs back then, as he gazes around at the sight, says, "I am glad I saw this. I promise we will never use such weapons again."

I stare at the man and the say, "Natalie would be proud of you, and all you have accomplished."

"Thank you," He says, then adds, "Oh, I also never did thank you for saving my life!"

I accept his words with a nod, and then watch as he boards the craft. I observe as the airship lifts off and begins its return journey. I wait until it is a distant speck in the sky before making my way to the devastated city's museum.

I make good time and, once there, recover Madcat's pelt from inside, drape it over my shoulders, and then begin my trek back to where I left the crates. Knowing that Madcat died of old age, rather than at the hands of some hunting party, brings me peace.

The late afternoon sky is clear, with the clouds having been whisked away by the mild breeze. The crates are where I left them, not surprising considering that there is no one around. I open one of the crates, remove a series of chains, some purpose made grass skis, and a harness. Setting the crates on the skis and chaining them together, does not take long. I carefully pack Madcat's pelt, put on the harness, and step in front of the first crate. I attach the chains to the harness, then lean forward, and pull. Getting the load to move takes all I have, but once the crates are sliding, I am able to keep forward momentum going without too much difficulty.

It is nightfall by the time I approach the cave. I slow my pace and search the area intently. There is no sign of the temporary bridges, nor of the armada that I saw when I was first roused from my pod. This pleases me greatly, as my task will be a lot easier. I use the cover of darkness to open the cave entrance, and then to transfer the crates inside.

Once I am done, I step out into the pale moonlight and gaze at the drag marks the sled made through the grass, and where I can clearly see my distinctive footprints with them. I decide to ignore them all, it is doubtful anyone will be in the area before the grass springs back into place.

I ceremoniously drape Madcat's pelt over one of the other pods, hook the new battery backup units to the craft's main power, and begin running system tests. Having sufficient power to launch; all that remains is to seal the gaping hole in the front. My excitement builds as I activate the crafts many systems. Internal gravity, life support, navigation, and more, all power up successfully.

An alarm blares from the console. The unexpected noise stops me in my tracks. I stare at the message displayed, then roar at the top of my lungs in frustration. I shut down the craft's systems and then stride to a nearby panel. The second I open it, acrid smoke spills out. I wave the smoke away and stare in disbelief at the burned-out circuits.

I glance at the opening in the front of the craft and recall all the thruster tests I conducted. Sighing, I realize that my failure to run the transport's life support, with its associated filter system, allowed dust to penetrate places it normally would not. I am now paying the price for my mistakes, and a high price that is. This craft is not going anywhere, not until I can replace the damaged control circuits, and that will require technology far beyond anything I have witnessed to date. I glance at my crafting tool, and then shake my head. The repairs required are far beyond even this tool's capabilities.

I consider my options for a few moments, and then finally do the only thing I can. I seal the cave's entrance and set my pod for a two-hundred-year sleep cycle. Hopefully the planet's technology will have advanced enough by then for me to be able to repair the damage. I glance at the new power units, and then, as a last-minute safeguard, hook one directly to the pod. Once I am satisfied that I have done all I can, I climb in and watch as the cover slides shut.

Chapter Five - Extraction

"How the hell did this Mamluk live for so long?" Asks a deep voice.

"I have no idea." Replies another man.

I slowly open my eyes, and gaze around, looking for the voices. My vision is blurred, and I feel sluggish, as though drugged. I am still inside my pod and am blocked from exiting by a latticework of some unfamiliar material. Not that I have the strength to even attempt to walk, let alone escape through the strange mesh.

A large shiny image comes into view. I force myself to concentrate and bring the object into focus. A man stands before me, wearing a full bodysuit, with only his visor open. He grins and says in his deep voice, "This one is toasted. We should be able to process it pretty easily."

"Yeah," replies a voice from somewhere behind me. The voice continues, "It took me a while to figure out this old unit, but I was able to set it to fifty percent recovery mode."

The man before me runs his gaze over my body, and exclaims, "Hey Zain, come and look at all these scars! This one has been through the wringer."

The other man responds hesitantly, "Hey Rand, hold up. Central wants this one alive, for testing and evaluation."

"Alive! Okay," Rand replies with a carefree shrug of his shoulders.

A second man walks into view; he too is wearing a full bodysuit made from some shiny metallic material. He stares at my pod for a moment, and then says, "We're getting chip data now." He reads the data from his visor, then whistles in surprise as he states, "Wow, this guy is ancient. According to its implant, it's a Gen five, and over two thousand years old!"

"I've never seen a Gen-Five before!" Rand states, "They're big!" he adds and then turns away from me as he inquires. "Hey Zain. Did you ever see the vid of that Gen-Seven? The one that dug its way out of the ship's hull."

"Uh, nope." Zain replies only half listening as he gazes around apprehensively. His eyes fall on a dust covered fur, Madcat's pelt. "What I am curious about is, what is that doing here?"

"Well I am more interested in finding out how that pod is still running. This transport is completely out of power!" Rand states incredulously.

Zain crouches down out of sight, and then after a few moments says, "Someone hooked up a backup power unit, and it's got wires leading to the main console!" The man stands and points to me and asks, "You don't think this thing did that, do you?"

"Don't worry," Rand comments as he shrugs his shoulders, "this guy is in suspended stasis, right?" As the man stares at me, he adds, "Besides it's obsolete, he can't do anything."

Zain turns back to his portable computer, and visibly staggers as he reads more information. He murmurs uneasily, "Wow! This one is from the Tyron Project."

"Emperor Tyron?" Rand questions doubtfully, barely catching the quietly spoken words.

"Yeah, an 'i' model." Zain continues warily as he turns to look at his colleague.

Rand's face twitches, and his mouth sounds dry as he comments "An infinite model. Oh crap!"

Zain turns back to his hand-held computer as he says, "I will see what the containment protocol is for a Tyron variant."

The other man shakes his head, "I can't believe that we're still cleaning up that mess."

"Well, the concept was a good one." Zain comments positively.

Rand scoffs, "Yeah right! Let's engineer the most efficient killing machine we can, and then program it to bond to an individual as their bodyguard."

"It worked, when it was done properly." Zain adds as he recalls a few incidents where Mamluks failed to follow their indoctrination.

"And when it doesn't, it falls on us to 'fix it'." He replies scornfully.

Zain rubs his short hair as he adds, "They also tended to go nuts when the person they were to protect died of old age, or due to some accident."

Rand shakes his head, "Do you still think it was a good idea?"

Zain shakes his head, and then glances at his beeping computer. He reads the information quickly, and then exclaims, "Oh crap. This one is already reported as processed."

Rand frowns and then lifts his hands questioningly as he asks, "Okay, and that means?"

Zain replies, "It means that someone with a lot of power made this guy's disappearance look like a successful sanitation."

"When?" Rand demands.

"Uh," Zain relaxes as he relays the date, "Seventy-five, seventy-eight. A hell of a long time ago."

I listen intently to every word the two men utter, but even so, the dates hold little meaning to me.

Rand rubs his chin as he ponders the ramifications of this, and then says, "Well hell. Let's just get this old boy to Central and let them deal with it."

I listen to their banter and evaluate what they are saying. The fact that I have a chip implanted somewhere in my body bothers me more than anything else. The rest of their story fills in a lot of gaps though. I consider their statement that I am to be returned alive, and then with my head clearing, weakly request, "Water."

Both men turn toward me, their eyes wide with fear.

Zain exclaims, "Bloody hell. It speaks!"

Rand glances left and right, then questions, "Do we have to bring it in alive?"

Zain sighs as he replies, "We can't kill it now, its chip will show that it was alive when we found it."

"Well if it weren't for that chip, we never would have found it when we entered orbit." Rand states in annoyance. He stares at me, aggravated, as he continues, "If our stupid system hadn't reported this discovery, we could have simply left it."

"Damn our luck," Zain agrees in exasperation, "this was supposed to be a simple survey mission."

Rand shakes his head as he leaves. He returns a moment later with an odd-looking pouch and then hands it to me through the mesh.

I stare at Rand's robust looking bodysuit, and the material which blocks my egress. I slowly lift my arm and take the pouch. I drink its contents, and instantly feel my strength returning. My mind is slowly clearing. I glance at the pod's controls then realize what is happening. The men may well have set the pod to fifty percent revival, but the backup power I installed, is completing the cycle, and reviving me fully.

Rand and Zain are standing over another pod, one they brought with them. They are blissfully unaware that I am regaining my strength. It is obvious that I am to be encased in the new pod, and then transported to wherever Central is. After a few moments they seem to be ready. Rand approaches me with a long needle and syringe.

I let my head slump as the man steps closer, feigning being weaker than I am. Though I am still a long way from being at full strength, it is obvious to me that I will only get one chance to escape. I close my secondary eye lids, hoping it makes me look sleepy.

Rand warily extends his hand with the needle through the mesh. I have no idea how strong the bodysuit is, so I resist the urge to immediately attack. His elbow crosses the mesh; the needle is almost touching my neck.

With lightning speed, I lift my hands, grab the needle and drive it into the only place I can. Straight into Rand's face. The needle penetrates the soft tissue of his eye, and easily slides deep inside. I inject the contents directly into his brain. He screams, spasms and twitches, and then falls to the ground, dead, the needle is grotesquely sticking out from his eye socket.

I shove with all my might, and successfully break through the mesh. Zain reaches for a sidearm of sorts, but never gets it. He stares at me perplexed; he seems unable to fathom why his hands are not working. His mouth opens, releasing vast quantities of blood. He falls to the ground, where he dies. My hand had slid into his faceplate on a downward angle, where my claws sliced his neck so deeply, I severed his spine.

I check the shuttle's power and find that its reserves are completely depleted. The only thing powering the console is a small portable unit which I presume the dead men installed, as it was not there when I entered my pod. I glance at the date and freeze. According to the data, I have been asleep for hundreds of years.

I slowly step outside the shuttle, and cautiously climb the rock wall I erected so long ago. I immediately see three more people, all wearing shiny bodysuits, working in the well-lit cavern. Under glow of powerful lights, they are clearing the entrance to my cave, making a direct path, rather than the s-bend which I built. The men seem oblivious to my presence as they casually work. I crouch down out of sight and reflect on why I was not woken up at the scheduled time. It then dawns on me that the circuit that failed must have affected my pod's master control timer.

I peek around the corner at the three men and scrutinize them. They all wear the same kind of bodysuits as the men I killed, complete with side arms, meaning that it will be difficult to take them all at once. As I deliberate my options, one of them stops, and looks in my direction. He taps his helmet, then pulls his weapon as he turns and speaks to his colleagues. I do not need to hear his words to know that he is going to investigate why he has lost contact with the men I killed.

I retreat into my shuttle and wait for the man. A moment passes before I can hear rocks sliding, indicating that someone has climbed the wall. I hear the footsteps plainly and wait for the man to step into the shuttle. His speed surprises me, but I am quicker, barely. I shove my hand, palm up, into his open faceplate. I drive my claws through his eyes then upward, into his brain. The man convulses and twitches, then as I retract my claws, he falls to the ground, dead. The weapon he drew now rests on the ground near my feet.

I turn to leave the shuttle and freeze at the sound of pebbles sliding and rolling outside. I listen intently, and although I hear nothing, I step backwards into the cockpit. The wall of the shuttle where I was standing begins to vibrate and oscillate. Suddenly it blows inward, leaving a massive hole in the side of the shuttle. I stare at the shredded wall, and then glance at the other side of the shuttle to find that it too, is a mangled mess.

A single footfall from outside the shuttle is all the warning I have and need. I step back as the wall next to me begins to vibrate, and then I drop to the floor a split second before it explodes inward, showering my back with shrapnel. I stare at the bodies of the men I killed earlier, and then spot a weapon. It is close, but may as well be on another planet, being on the far side of the open hatchway. I slink further back into the cockpit and consider my options.

A chill runs through my body at the sound of a metallic boot stepping into the shuttle. I glance at the large cracks around the central window panel I replaced long ago and consider my options. At the sound of a second footfall, I make my decision. There is no way that I can face off against two assailants who carry weapons that can virtually vaporize metal. I leap at the crumbling repairs, and cringe when the makeshift window holds, and instead of falling out, merely creaks and groans. I slam all my weight into it a second time as my peripheral vision catches sight of two people in metallic bodysuits lifting up their weapons. This time, momentum saves me as my sheer bulk and weight finally causes the panel to fall away. I tumble outside, and to the ground, just as the windows on either side explode outward, showering the area with hundreds of shards of glass. Miraculously I am spared the brunt of the glass shower, with only a few pieces harmlessly bouncing off my thick scales. I roll to the side, then swiftly rise and sprint for the wall that blocks the shuttle from the main cavern.

I leap over the top of the wall at full speed, oblivious to any danger on the other side. My adrenaline is running high from being so heavily outmatched. I have never before felt as outclassed as I do now, not even when I was tied to the tree, or being tortured. I skid and slide down the far slope and am thankful the cavern is unoccupied, but I fear that will change any second.

I rush outside, and into the unexpected darkness of night. The pale moon is partially blocked by clouds, allowing my egress to go largely unnoticed. I slide to a stop, digging long grooves in the ground with my rear claws. A person in a bodysuit stands in front of a ramp to a spacecraft, a mere fifty paces away, looking around. The vessel the person is standing guard over has sleek lines, and is easily four times the size of the transport I arrived in.

They turn, spot me, and immediately raise a small weapon. I do not hesitate, and dive to one side. I experience on odd sensation flowing across my side and feel a half dozen scales peel off my body. Now that was a close shave!

I stop, dig my heels into the ground once more, and spring backward as powerfully as I can, narrowly avoiding another shot by the strange weapon. I dive, jump, roll, and sprint in short bursts as I get ever closer to the weapon.

I have no idea why my attacker hesitates, but the brief respite is all I need to close the last few steps unopposed. I grab the arm with the weapon, and twist with all my might. Amazingly, instead of doing the expected, the arm turns towards me, the weapon inching closer every second. I let go of the arm as I drop down, then leap headlong through the open hatchway, and into the craft. I attempt to roll as I hit the deck, but instead slide into the far wall. The person turns toward me and lowers their weapon. The two from the cave are running toward the craft, but they too, do not fire.

As I stand, I glance to the sides of the open hatch and grin as I imagine their expressions when I close the doorway. Their unwillingness to risk damaging the craft is quite telling, perhaps this is their only one? Looking around I see an arrangement of chairs, side tables, along with matte black display panels. The rear of the craft leads to an area with a half dozen bunks, some of which are folded up into recesses. A single doorway with unusual markings on it rests in the rear of this area.

Quickly moving forward, I stride into the cockpit area and see two chairs before a pair of consoles. The consoles are matte black, like those in the entry area. I touch one of the panels and smile when it activates and lights up. I examine the series of symbols and controls, for a moment, slightly perplexed. The controls are similar to the craft in my cave, yet different enough to cause me to pause.

A slight swoosh sound, accompanied by a small change in air pressure, reaches my ears. The door is open!

I scan the console quickly, then as I hear the clomping of feet on the deck plates, I stab at a familiar control. The craft responds instantly, launching off the ground, and hovering. I turn and face the pair who made it on board, and say, "What are you going to do now?"

They lift their dark visors, then look at each other. Clearly, they did not expect me to speak.

One of the suit wearers is female; she probes, "What are you?"

"I am Mamluk," I reply proudly, then without any hesitation, step forward and drive my hands into both of their open faceplates, killing them instantly.

As they fall to the ground another intruder steps into view and lifts his weapon. He fires point blank at my chest. I expect my life to end, but instead the man screams, "Stupid safeties!"

He hurls the weapon at me, then quickly retreats toward the rear of the craft. I stride after the man, and as he opens the door with the symbols on it, I wrench him back. He puts his hands up and begs, "Please don't kill me. I'll do anything!"

"Remove your armor!" I demand.

The man hesitantly complies. The front opens with an audible hiss, allowing him to step out. I stare at the armor, appreciative of its elegant and functional design. Its outer casing is exceedingly thin, while the inside is filled with a sponge-like substance which fully encases the wearer's arms, legs, and body. I stare at the material and consider its purpose. Perhaps it relays muscle stimuli.

I point to the bodysuit and ask, "How is it that your armor is so thin, and yet so strong?"

The petrified man replies, "Our scientists discovered a new polymer. Also, if you look carefully on the inside edge you will see a layer of self-repairing gelatin. They work in conjunction, and we apply it to all armor and..." The man abruptly stops talking, and stares at me with wide eyes.

He was about to share something and, although he is scared, has the presence of mind not to give me all the information he has. I smile at the quivering man, which obviously adds to his anxiety. I know he will tell me everything I need to know, in time.

As I stare at the man's upturned face it dawns on me that all these people have the same eyes, a rich hazel, flecked with rainbow of other colors, creating a sparkling effect.

"How many of you were on this ship?" I demand.

"Just the five of us." The man whimpers back.

"And in orbit?" I demand with a scowl.

"Oh, there is a full strike force in orbit." The man replies sullenly, realizing that if I have no escape, then more than likely nor does he.

"Okay," I respond slowly, resisting the urge to kill the man. "Now, be more specific. What is a full strike force?" I am becoming increasingly frustrated with his replies.

The man gulps, then, while his face twitches, he replies, "A Pathfinder survey craft, three Arbiter class cruisers, and one command carrier."

I frown at the man's answer, and then ask, "That sounds like a lot of effort to retrieve me."

"Oh, we didn't know you were here, until we arrived in orbit, anyway." He replies resentfully.

"Well, if you did not come for me, what are you here for?" I ask, pressing the man for more information.

"We're here to evaluate the planet for sterilization prior to colonization." He replies blandly, as if this were a routine endeavor.

I consider the inhabitants of this planet, and then realize that they should have advanced their technologically during my slumber. I grab the man and lead him to the front of the craft and say, "Show me an aerial view of the planet, particularly the island chain past those canyons."

The man swallows hard but complies. Within seconds I am staring at a city in ruins. I lift my hand to the man, who shields his body as he cries out, "That wasn't us!"

I stare at the destruction in more detail and can indeed see that the area shows signs of encroaching vegetation, while the collapsed bridges are caked with rust and appear to have been disused for many years.

The man cautiously ventures, "Our orbital scans indicated that this event occurred hundreds of years ago." The man gains a little confidence and continues, "We have seen it before. Jealous, lesser advanced cultures gang up and eliminate the more advanced culture by sheer weight of numbers. It's a pity really, because they invariably fail to capture the technology they seek, and in fact, reverse the planet's overall technological growth." He shrugs and then looks at me with a resigned expression. It is obvious, he expects die soon.

I turn to the man and say, "If I live, so will you, you have my word!"

"How can I trust you?" He scoffs, then steps back, immediately regretting his harsh comment.

"Because I am Mamluk!" I state, as if that were all the answer he needs.

The man's face twitches for a moment as he decides what to do. Finally, he replies, "My name is Yoloth, Yoloth McKenzie." He hesitates once more, and then reluctantly asks, "What would you have me do?"

I motion to the console and simply state, "Show me!"

The man steps toward the console, then apprehensively shows me the ship's controls. It does not take me long to realize that this craft is not too different from the one I first woke in. It becomes clearer and clearer to Yoloth that I understand a lot more than he thought I did, and he begins to expand his tutorial. Once he is done, I stare at the controls and grin.

I touch the panel, activating the shields, and then after a brief pause, take us upward. The craft accelerates swiftly and silently though the clouds, and into space. I find the craft's controls easy to use, and responsive.

Yoloth stammers, "Oh crap. That's the Command Carrier, and it's on an intercept course." I glance at the man, and then follow his finger to the main viewer. A small blimp is in the distance, getting larger as it approaches.

I glance at the system scanner and can see the other ships in various positions around the planet, leaving the Carrier as the only ship between us and freedom.

A blight flare-like blast unexpectedly impacts against the craft. The energy spreads around the ship, and based on the system's status report, does no damage.

I turn to my captive, unimpressed, and state, "Weak weapon for an all-powerful race!"

Yoloth lowers his gaze as he mumbles, "That was not an offensive strike, they're draining our shields."

I glance back at the craft's systems once more, and notice that the shield energy is at eighty percent, and slowly diminishing. I cast my gaze over the console and then, finding what I am looking for, stab at the weapons control. The control flickers, but nothing obvious happens.

The Carrier is close enough that I can see some of its details. It is a monstrous cigar shaped spacecraft with hundreds of portholes indicating at least thirty levels. I stare at it for a moment, and then stop cold. I am stunned. A gaping hole has been blasted completely through it! As the ship turns, I can see gas and debris venting into space from both the entry and exit holes.

"They're going to shoot back now!" Yoloth states dejectedly. He curls up on the floor in a fetal position and begins to whimper.

I immediately put us into a crazed series of erratic maneuvers. I am suddenly thrown to the deck as the sound of metal tearing reaches my ears. The controls flash warnings of systems failures and extensive hull damage. Miraculously, the pilot area is still intact. I glance at the controls and see that the shields are down, as is main power. Most of the thrusters are out of commission and reserve energy is nearly depleted.

The craft is spiraling out of control and heading straight for the rear of the massive carrier. The lights flicker as the power cuts out, and then comes back on. The Carrier is so close I can see the individual launch ramps, presumably for its fighters, and there are hundreds of them lining the axis of the craft. As we drift behind the Carrier, I can make out its main engines, and their associated support structures. I glance at the control board, and wince at the imminent 'complete systems failure' warning. I stare ahead and, then utilizing all the ship has left, aim between the support struts of one of the Carrier's main drive units. The ship is still tumbling when we impact, causing the craft to twist around cruelly as we become wedged.

Yoloth cries out in fear at the sound of tearing metal, and then once we stop, he returns to his curled-up position, and whimpers once more.

I ignore the man as I review the mangled ship's systems. Main power is out, as is the main drive, and the gravity lift system. Secondary power is also out of commission, and with it, the thrusters, long range sensors, and numerous other lesser systems. All that is left is the emergency reserve, which will run the life support, and the shortrange sensors, along with a distress beacon. I immediately confirm that the beacon is off, and then decide to shut everything down, including life support. The craft becomes deathly quiet as everything shuts down. The gravity plating would seem to be an independent system, as it remains functional.

A flash of light from outside catches my attention. Unbelievably the Carrier would appear to have activated its main drive. A faint noise from the console gets my attention. The secondary power is back online, as are a few of the lesser systems.

I turn to the frightened man and ask, "Do you know how it is that the secondary power is now working, when it was showing as damaged before?"

Yoloth stops whimpering, then quickly stands and rushes to the console. I watch cautiously as he reviews the panel. He suddenly grins widely, then laughs manically as he slaps my arm. He quickly pulls his hand away and shakes it. My scales seem to have stung his hand.

I have waited long enough for a reply, and demand, "What is it?"

Yoloth motions outside as he explains, "The Carrier's commander must have decided that we were destroyed and is now heading for a repair facility." He smiles and then points to the console as he continues, "And out of sheer luck, this craft has an auto-repair feature, and it's active. With secondary power now operational, we should have limited propulsion back online in no time."

"It looks as though I get to keep my promise to you!" I state candidly.

The man appears confused, so I reiterate, "You may yet live!"

He grins, stares at me strangely, and then asks fearfully, "How am I to explain my presence on this ship?"

"First things first." I reply, and then add, "We need to see where we end up, and then come up with a plan."

Arrival

As suddenly as we began moving, we slow. A brief shudder runs through the ship as we transition to a near stop. The Carrier begins to make a slow roll, revealing an enormous space station, one with dozens of spacecraft docked to it.

I consider my plight and then venture, "We must get this ship clear of the support struts."

Yoloth hesitates for a moment, and then decides to assist. He taps on the console and displays a computer-generated image of our craft's position. In a show of great skill and prowess he slowly pilots the craft out from between the struts. He begins to sweat as the craft becomes lodged, then frees itself.

I look up as the grating sound of tearing metal reverberates through the craft. With a final lurch, we are free. I gaze at the screen in awe. The Carrier is enormous, we were literally wedged between the support struts belonging to a single engine, and as we move away, I see a second engine, then a third. In all, the Carrier has seven engines in three rows.

"Oh no!" Yoloth exclaims glumly. He points to a distant dot, one that is getting larger every second, "they must be looking for us!"

"Shut everything down!" I demand.

He hesitates, but then complies. Inertia keeps us drifting past the rear of the massive Carrier. I notice Yoloth's horrified expression, then look up to see that we have drifted directly behind one of the Carrier's main engines, where deep inside I see a bright glow. I consider firing the craft's weapon but realize that would probably be suicide.

Fortunately, the Carrier uses is thrusters as it moves away. As it approaches the Space station, the scale of its size becomes daunting, even to me. The enormous Carrier, though the largest vessel in the area, is still small in comparison to the Space Station.

Yoloth points at the screen and says, "They're ignoring us! I can't believe that the area's tracking station has not picked us up.

"Tracking Station?" I query

"Yes. They are everywhere and monitor all space traffic." He replies automatically.

I stare at various ships which are docked to the Space Station and as an idea comes to mind ask, "Is there any way we can get a passive scan of those ships?"

"Sure!" Yoloth replies. He then hesitantly asks, "But, how do I know you will let me live, once I have done all you ask?"

I stare at the man for a moment, and then finally reply, "You either trust my word, or you do not. The choice is yours."

He sighs despondently, then taps the console, revealing the data on all the ships present. Clearly, he has decided to either trust me, or at least understands that if he fails to assist, he will die. Either way, I do not care, so long as he does as requested.

I read the data on the various spacecraft when suddenly one of them gets my attention. I stare at the manifest and feel a chill rising at what I see. I had no idea there were so many of us. I review the information on the transport and its cargo, and then formulate a plan.

I turn to Yoloth and state, "You will live!"

Epilogue

"This is tracking station LJW 148876, please repeat your last transmission." The young girl stares at her screen nervously. She had heard the message quite clearly but cannot accept it.

A frantic voice almost shouts out, "I am standing at the airlock, and I am telling you, it's gone!"

The girl shakes her head in disbelief as she asks, "Are you at the right airlock?"

"Yes, I am at the right airlock!" The young man replies in exasperation.

"How can you lose a class nine transport?" She says more to herself, than the young man.

"I don't know," replies the youth in desperation.

"Was anything on it?" She enquires almost half-heartedly as she taps her fingers on the desk. She knows that a class nine is reserved for military transports, and they do not always disclose their cargo.

A few seconds later the boy whimpers his response, and as he does so the hairs on the back of her neck stand up. "Three thousand five hundred, generation seven Mamluks, in stasis."

"Three thousand five hundred," she repeats slowly, then in a fearful whisper wonders aloud, "Where'd they go?"

"That's what I'm trying to tell you. The computer says the ship is docked, but I am right here, and it's not." The boy gulps then states, "My career is over; I'll be lucky if I don't spend the rest of my days locked up, or worse."

The girl frowns as she hears an airlock cycling, then nothing. She asks uneasily, "Are you there?"

Silence is her only reply.

With shaky fingers, she logs the incident, then waits for Protectorate Security to show up. She has heard stories and rumors of the Mamluk project, and if any of them are true, no one is safe. She stands and walks to a viewport, then gazes out. In the distance lies the massive Space Station where the transport is supposed to be. She considers the space-junk she reported earlier, debris from the Carrier was her assessment, and then wonders.

Mystery Solved

Meanwhile, on the missing Transport…

Yoloth stares up at me with mild trepidation, and says, "Mamluk, I have done all that you have asked of me."

"Yes, you have," I reply. Then add questioningly, "How is it that you made this entire transport invisible to the sensors?"

"Oh, I used to work for ASP, Atlan Special Purpose branch. They do a lot of things on the quiet." He replies boastfully.

"But the entire transport?" I press. "It's really invisible to all sensors?""Yes!" Yoloth replies, "Even the periphery tracking stations can't see this vessel."

"How is that possible?" I ask, doubting his boasts.

"Military transports are pre-equipped with the capability; you just have to have the right access codes." Yoloth replies with a shrug.

I nod my head as I state, "Ah. That makes sense." I glance around and then add, "Well, I gave you my word that you would live. And so you shall. You may leave in a shuttle at any time."

Yoloth frowns, and then asks, "You know these Mamluks you picked up have limited life spans, right?"

"Yes, I do!" I state with a toothy grin smile.

"What are you going to do with them?" Yoloth asks, a little too boldly.

"Oh, I have a plan!" I reply, and then motion for Yoloth to be on his way.

"I have a plan!" I repeat to myself quietly.

Beyond the Protectorate

Staring at the bulkhead ahead fills me with rage. I have learned much from this military transport's database. There seems to be no limit to the information it carries. I slam my fist onto my table. What the Atlan Protectorate has done to my kind is unconscionable. We would have become the masters and rulers of our planet and our own destiny, but that has forever been denied to us. Instead, we have been genetically altered to become throw away soldiers for a compassionless empire.

My emergence as a free thinking Mamluk would seem to be unique. From what I have read, none of my kind has ever received the training that I have, but that is going to change. With thirty-five hundred, of my species now being trained, as I was, things will never go back to the way they were for my kind.

I lift my gaze to Madcat's pelt, which adorns my wall, and proclaim, "I will exact revenge on the Protectorate for what they have done, I swear it!"

###

I hope you have enjoyed reading 'Mamluk', as much as I have enjoyed writing it. Please remember to leave a review, so that others may read your thoughts on this story.

For more information about my other works, please head over to www.landsofphrey.com, or www.terranchronicles.com.

To keep in touch, join the Terran Chronicles Universe or Lands of Phrey Facebook pages and follow me on Twitter @JamesAJJackson

James Jackson